Mountain Justice

by

Harley Herrald

Copyright © 2003 by Harley Herrald
All Rights Reserved

This is a work of fiction. All characters are fictional and any resemblance to persons living or dead is purely coincidental.

No part of this book may be reproduced in any form whatsoever, whether by graphic, visual, electronic, filming, microfilming, tape recording, or any other means, without the written permission of the author, except in the case of brief passages embodied in critical reviews and articles where the title, author and ISBN accompany such review or article.

Published and Distributed by:

Granite Publishing and Distribution, LLC
868 North 1430 West
Orem, Utah 84057
(801) 229-9023 • Toll Free (800) 574-5779
Fax (801) 229-1924

Page Layout & Design by Myrna Varga • The Office Connection, Inc.
Cover Design by Tammie Ingram
Cover Art by Jennett Chandler

ISBN: 1-930980-97-3
Library of Congress Control Number: 2002117633
Printed in the United States of America

10 9 8 7 6 5 4 3 2 1

*To those who read and remember
and, also, to those who
read and wonder.*

Chapter 1

There are only two things worse than lying to yourself: lying to someone else and lying about anyone.

As I sit here on the mountainside, looking down at the cluster of buildings that have become the center of my life, I can't help wondering about myself.

I had come into this country broke, friendless, and alone. I am now more than I had ever dreamed I might become.

But now, I wonder if all I think I own, and have become, is only a house of cards that could crash down around my ears at any moment.

It is true, I am now what was referred to as, "a respected member of the community." I owe no one, I have property, and my wife and I possess a degree of wealth. I present myself as a lawyer, even presuming to refer to myself occasionally as an attorney. I have friends, family, and yes, even those who seem to hang on my every word. But when I stand in front of a mirror shaving every morning, I can hardly meet my own gaze.

I am not so much ashamed as I am worried I might be found out. Few know, and fewer guess what one thinks when one feels unworthy of what he has and has become.

Oh, I've worked and studied hard to get wherever it is I am. I came into this valley as a grub-line riding cowboy, out of work, practically broke, and at least three hundred miles from anyone I might call a friend.

I met, worked for, and finally married my Clatilda. It was because of her ranch and her money that I have been able to get to where I am. Some, even, resent my achievements. I cannot deny that what I am is not solely due to my own efforts. These are facts I live with daily.

Soon, though, all will see me for what I really am.

I have been asked to serve as a circuit judge for the southern part of the Colorado Territory. This will include the country from Trinidad to Durango. And, I must give an answer by Monday, next. Six more days, and if I agree, I begin the task of exposing my ignorance and lack of ability to almost one fourth of an entire territory. I will sit across the bench from men smarter, better educated, and better read in the law than I can ever hope to be. It will certainly not take long for all to recognize and identify my woeful lack of knowledge, and even my buffoonery.

I have been at my profession for only a few short years. Each day I, once again, discover how little I know. What's more difficult are those things I must remember. As a cowboy, range conditions, water and livestock never changed much. Oh, weather can affect everything, but last year's winter would not dictate the snowfall this year. Bad cattle prices are to be forgotten, and not referred in a way to directly influence the future.

Now I often find myself with my head abuzz with citations and references to cases in the past, bearing upon a case with which I may be currently involved.

Whoever nominated me for this job must have been severely fooled, but how I don't know.

Chapter 2

I was still no closer to a decision when I started down off the mountain. I had prayed, worried and stewed for almost two weeks and still had no answer.

As I rode around the barn, I was met by my Uncle Buck and my son, Bud.

"Pa," Bud said when he saw me, "Judge Nava, from Alamosa, is in the house. Ma says he wants to see you. She sent me and Uncle Buck to fetch you."

As I handed Bud the reins to my horse, I wondered that I had not seen Jamie ride into the yard.

My wife, Clatilda, met me at the door. "Will, Judge Nava has been here for almost two hours. We were about to give up on you."

I went into the dining room to find my old friend sitting at the table. From the array of dishes, it appeared he had already had his dinner.

"Jamie!" I said, reaching for his extended hand. "How are you, and what brings you here?"

"I'm fine, Will, and I come on a double errand. I can see you're looking fit and prosperous!"

"The fitness and look both come from Clatilda. She seems to feel it is my obligation to earn my keep, and on this ranch, it's not hard to find work. The seemingly prosperous look is also her doing. She says that if, in addition to being a cowhand, I wish to practice law, I must at least keep my boots clean. In all honesty I sometimes long for dirty boots. But, now, what is the reason for your most welcome visit?"

I sat down across the table from Jamie while Clatilda placed a glass of cold milk in front of me and a plate of cookies between us.

"As I said, Will, I have two reasons for being here. The first is to owns up to my complicity in what Clatilda tells me is the problem you've been wrestling the past two weeks. The second is an errand on behalf of the governor, no less. I must confess it was I who suggested you as a candidate for the office that seems to be causing you so much worry and concern. I really felt you would want the position. It was definitely not my intent to create problems for you."

"So you're the scoundrel who thinks I'm smart enough to be a circuit judge! Jamie, how, in your wildest imagination, could you think me capable to sit as a judge? Man, you've seen me in your own courtroom at least four dozen times in the past few years. You've been witness to the stupid mistakes I'm capable of making. I don't believe that kind, or even as many, mistakes would be tolerated of a judge."

"Oh ho! So that's it. All the way up here I have been trying to figure out why we have not heard from you. I knew it was not like you to delay a decision for so long, but, I never figured you would be having an attack of the 'poor little me'."

"Will, I've watched you for the past few years grow into the best attorney I've ever seen. Oh, sure you make a few honest mistakes, never a stupid one and never the same one twice. Man, is it your belief a judge never makes a mistake? If that's so, then your opinion of me must be low indeed! We're not machines, Will. We're just folks. You are more qualified to be a judge than any man I know, and that does include me. Your knowledge of the law is much better than you think, and what's more, you're the most honest man I know."

"Well. I do thank you, sir, for that, but I still can't see me as a judge."

"That brings me to the final reason for my visit. Judge Claus, whose retirement was the reason for the offer made to you, was killed last Friday when his buggy slipped over the edge of a wash down by Durango. The governor wants you in Trinidad this coming Monday for the court session. I'm to wire him of your decision no later than day after tomorrow night."

Well, there it is, I thought. No more fooling around. Now's the time to fish or cut bait.

"Will," Clatilda said, "I've said nothing for the past two weeks, but this is something for which you have worked very hard, and cowboy, it's time!"

I looked over at this woman that, over the years, had been so much for and to me, this lady who had born my children as well as my foolishness. She'd been there when I was physically hurt, when I did well, and also when I did poorly. She supported all of my actions, and in her advice to me had been, without fail, equally honest and right.

"Jamie, tell the governor that I'll be at the Trinidad Courthouse Monday morning, bright and early."

"Well, finally!" Uncle Buck snorted from the front door.

I looked over my shoulder to see him, Jacob, and Bud, standing just inside the door. All grinning like a trio of Cheshire cats.

"The whole family in on this?" I asked of all and no one in particular.

"Of course we are, Will. Would you think it would be any other way?" Clatilda asked. "I've practically had to sit on Uncle Buck for this last week. He's kept saying you needed to be 'sternly spoken to'."

I sat there looking at Jamie with what I was sure was a right stupid grin on my face.

"You know, my friend, I'm not sure the real decision was ever rightly mine. It appears that everyone but me had their minds long since made up."

"Yeah," Jamie answered, "and partner, I just can't quite get myself to feel sorry for you. Well, Judge Jackson, I will advise the governor of your decision. I don't know who he will send, but someone will meet you in Trinidad with your commission, I would imagine the same person will swear you into your new office, and of course, I wouldn't miss being there for the world! Now, let me be the first to congratulate you, Judge!" Jamie said, standing, with his bear-paw of a hand extended across the table.

It was with a great deal of misgivings that I shook Jamie's hand.

Jamie excused himself, refusing Clatilda's offer for him to stay for supper, saying he must hurry back to Alamosa so he could get his wire off to the governor advising him of my decision.

There was very little work done the rest of that day. Too much celebrating. Clatilda even insisted upon inviting the Blalocks, our neighbors, to supper. Anne Blalock arrived within minutes after Bud returned from extending the invitation. She walked straight up to me and planted a big kiss right on my cheek.

"Will Jackson!" she said, stepping back from me, still holding my shoulders, "all this time I never thought you'd amount to a hill of beans, now you go make a liar of me. Imagine me hugging a judge!"

Whereupon, she did exactly that. She grabbed and hugged me with such ferocity I wasn't sure if either of us would survive. And all this time that wife of mine just stood there with a smile on her face, fit to light up the darkest night.

Clatilda, Anna Laura and Anne busied themselves with preparing supper while Jacob, Uncle Buck and Bud gathered around me as if I was someone important who had come to visit. It was all more than a little embarrassing. It was even more so when Seth Blalock and his two boys arrived with their round of congratulations.

After supper, the ladies decided that the entire families, both mine and the Blalocks, would go with me to Trinidad to witness my swearing-in. We decided to leave Jim Ballard and his wife to care for the ranch. Jim had worked for us for several years and was well suited to care for the place, plus his wife was expecting their second child any day and would not be up to the trip. By the time the plans were all completed, I had finally extracted a promise from my old friend, Jacob Webber, that he would leave at least most of the arsenal he regularly carried on his person, at home. It was late and we were all tired, so bed that night was most welcome.

Come morning everyone was up early, for there was much to be done to get ready for the trip to Trinidad. The usual packing and the last minute details to be seen about the ranch. Jim Ballard was sorry not to be going to Trinidad with us, but he was proud that I would leave him in charge of the ranch. He seemed concerned he could care for the operation.

It was late that night when finally we were in bed. Clatilda turned to me, "Will, do I now call you 'Judge Cowboy' or 'Cowboy Judge'?"

I'm pretty sure she loves me, but I've never been real sure of her respect for my position in the legal community.

Chapter 3

Thursday morning dawned bright and clear, and found us already on the road, well beyond our little village. Cold, but good traveling weather. We decided to go all the way to Alamosa without stopping. It would put us into Alamosa in the middle of the night, but we had a lot of country to cover before Monday morning. We made quite a caravan. Bud drove our surrey, stuffed with luggage and my folks. Seth drove his surrey, also full with his folks and their baggage. Jacob, Uncle Buck and I were horseback. Bud would have preferred to ride with Uncle Buck and Jacob, but I needed the time alone. I would enjoy horseback. I needed time to think more of what I was getting into. I had only appeared before three judges, as a lawyer, including Jamie Nava. Once, before Judge Claus, whom I was replacing, and once before a Judge Kerner, in Gunnison. Jamie, of course, was my friend. And while I knew he would cut me but little slack in his courtroom, he was, nevertheless still my friend. I tried to remember my impression of Judge Claus and I could only remember that, in fact, he'd made little or no impression upon me. Judge Kerner, in Gunnison, had seemed to be more caught up in himself, than in the law. Even to the point of not allowing anyone at his table during dinner or supper, except one or two local politicians. I hoped, somehow to be like none of the three. Sterner than Jamie, more positive than Claus and in no way like Kerner. At least, as a judge.

We appeared more as movers, than folks on an excursion. We got into Alamosa right at midnight but it was well after one in the morning before everyone was settled down.

I had thought Clatilda would be worn out, and go right to sleep, but she insisted on talking for almost an hour after we went to sleep. It seemed that on the trip down she had suddenly realized just how much my new endeavor would keep me from the ranch. She felt it necessary we should settle what was to be done, and by whom, in my future absences. I suggested we might discuss this at a later time. Such was not to be the case. By the time we went to sleep that night it was settled that Jacob and Uncle Buck would run the ranch, Bud would continue his schooling, helping on the ranch when not in school, and Clatilda and the twins would accompany me, when possible. And when this would not be possible, it was clear a lot of complaining would go on. Anna Laura would be finishing her schooling, and in the tender mercies of Anne Blalock in Clatilda's absences. The remainder of the trip into Trinidad was rough but we arrived late Sunday afternoon, thus affording all a good night's sleep.

As we all walked to the court house Monday morning, I felt much as a condemned man. My friends and family had offered much encouragement over a leisurely breakfast but nothing could quiet the feeling that I was about to get in far over my head and should, soon, make a grand fool of myself.

When we reached the court house steps, a vaguely familiar looking man disengaged himself from a small crowd and came toward us.

"And, this would be the new Judge!" he said, stepping up in front of me.

"Yes, sir," I said, "I am Will Jackson, but sir, your name escapes me, though your face is quite familiar."

"I'm not surprised you don't remember me, sir. It's been a while. I am Judge Wheeler from Denver; Thomas Wagner's brother-in-law. We met only the one time when you were shopping for your library. I have come, at the governor's request, to administer the oath of your office to you, Judge Jackson."

"Of course! I am sorry Judge Wheeler. I certainly should have remembered you, sir! Most particularly after all of your help. Please remember to give my warmest regards to Judge Wagner, when next you see him."

"You may do that, yourself, sir. He is standing at your other elbow."

I turned to have one shoulder grabbed by Judge Wagner and with his other hand he clasped mine and smiling as I had never seen him, he looked me right in the eye.

"Well, cowboy, how does it feel to reach your highest goal?"

"Sir, I feel totally unworthy!"

"Ha! Is this the same man who, after only studying Blackstone's Comments for a few months, saw through two cases as if through a clear window?"

I couldn't answer. I just stood as if rooted to the ground.

"Come on, Will, let me and Ralph Wheeler lead you as a lamb to the slaughter!"

I looked quickly at him to see him smiling at Judge Wheeler.

"Judge Jackson," Wheeler said, "do you believe yourself to be the only man to be frightened out of his wits, upon being asked to sit on the bench. I can remember when I was asked to take such a position. I didn't sleep for five days and nights and did not eat for three. I tried to drink a glass of milk the morning I was to be sworn in. I couldn't even keep that down. I was afraid the first cub lawyer to appear before me would laugh me off the bench!"

"Do you really ever get over that feeling, sir?" I asked.

"Not really! The first time I was able to slap down a smart mouthed young lawyer, I felt like a God. Then that very afternoon an even younger lawyer made me appear as a fool with a citation I never dreamed existed. Stay humble, Jackson, stay humble. That's the best advise I can give you, and I might add, the most difficult to follow. Right, Thomas?" he said looking to Judge Wagner.

"That, and one other thing," Judge Wagner said, his hand still on my shoulder, "don't ever forget what I told you about the three types of lawyers, Will. The cynic, the greed driven, and the buffoon."

"Oh, ha!" Judge Wheeler said, "I see you've been treated to Thomas' lawyer types? Just remember some are shades of two or more of those types. Watch and study, Will, watch and study!"

My family and friends had stood back while all this had been going on, but were soon dragged into the circle when Judge Wheeler welcomed Clatilda, then there were the many introductions.

Thomas Wagner looked twice when he was introduced to Jacob.

"Shot anyone lately, Mr. Webber?" he asked.

"Nope, ain't been shot at much either."

They laughed together as two old friends.

I harkened back to Uncle Buck's trouble in Cimarron when thieves had tried to steal his property. A situation finally settled by this same Judge Wagner.

When Judge Wagner shook Uncle Buck's hand, Uncle Buck looked him right in the eye and as calm as a Sunday morning in June, said right out; "Ain't been shot myself lately Judge, but thanks to my niece, Mrs. Jackson, here, I spent last evening reading the Denver paper, left in our hotel lobby by some traveler. Read it cover to cover."

"Well, Mr. Jackson, I can think of few things that please me more. Good for you, and the fine lady."

I'm sure Thomas Wagner was no where near as pleased to hear Uncle Buck say he could read, as Uncle Buck had been to tell him. For, the last time they had met, Uncle Buck not only could not read, he couldn't even sign his own name. He could, then, only make his mark.

Introductions complete, Judge Wheeler suggested we go on into the court house for the ceremonies.

When he said that, my blood ran cold for I could see no way, but to go through with it.

We walked into a courtroom, nearly full of people.

Some were obviously attorneys or politicians for they were inside the rail that separated the audience from the court itself. All seemed eager to shake my hand and introduce themselves.

Finally, I had enough. I stepped closer to the bench and turned to face the crowd.

"I am pleased to meet you all, but please understand it will be days, even weeks before I put a face to a name. Please let me get to know all of you as time dictates. For now, I'll just thank you for your well wishes and let's get on with whatever we are here to do."

"Well said, sir!" Judge Wheeler said standing beside me. "If we can get a Bible, we'll get on with offering you the oath of office."

Clatilda stood and motioned to me. I stepped over and she handed me two books.

"Here, Will, use both of these."

As I returned to Judge Wheeler, I could see Clatilda had given me our family Bible and my old, well worn, Book of Mormon.

I handed both to Judge Wheeler. He glanced at the Book of Mormon.

Quietly he said, so that only I could hear, "Will, I think this to be most appropriate."

Without further ado, he called for quiet, then he offered me the oath of my office. After which he handed me a rolled up paper which proved to be my commission signed by some I had never heard of, with the exception of the governor.

I looked up, after taking my commission, and the two books, from Judge Wheeler, and there stood Jamie Nava.

He gently stepped between Judge Wheeler and me.

"Excuse me, Judge, but I claim the right to be the first to shake Judge Jackson's hand."

He not only shook my hand but he enveloped me in a huge bear-hug.

When Jamie stepped back, Thomas Wagner stepped up.

"Will, if I can't be first, I demand to be next."

He took my hand in both of his, looking me right in the eye.

"Will, I've heard from many of your honesty, and I personally know of your quick mind. Lose neither!"

After that, for the next ten or fifteen minutes, things were a blur of well wishers, family, and lawyers. The latter seeming to sharply divide themselves into two groups; those fawning over me as if I were the belle of the ball, and others who seemed more to be simply doing their duty.

After things had somewhat settled down, a rather smallish man, completely bald, shyly approached.

"Judge Jackson, I am J.W. Fisher. I served Judge Claus as his clerk and recorder. I would hope to serve you in the same capacity." He said offering me a hand; not large but with the longest fingers I'd ever seen.

Judge Wheeler and Judge Wagner were standing beside me.

"Will, you will need to have a clerk and recorder. Yours is to be a court of record and, as such, one like Mr. Fisher will be required."

"Who will he be working for and who will pay him?" I asked.

"He will work for you, but the state will pay him," Judge Wheeler responded.

"If he don't make a hand, then can I replace him?"

"I assume you mean if he doesn't do good work?" Wheeler asked.

"That's what I mean."

"He will serve at your pleasure."

"That means I can fire him?"

"Yes."

"Then Mr. Fisher, you're hired! Now you tell me; what comes first?"

"I have a docket of the cases pending before this court. You may chose to hear them in whatever order you please."

"Do you have the dates these cases were filed?"

"Yes, sir, both civil and criminal."

"Then, Mr. Fisher, my family, these three gentlemen: referring to the Judges Wheeler, Wagner and Nava, and I will go over to the hotel and have a little refreshment, then I'll be back and we will begin with the oldest case first."

"The oldest case is a murder case. Given the late start, what with the dinner adjournment, may be you'd like to start with one of the smaller cases."

"Mr. Fisher; may I call you J.W.?"

"Certainly, sir."

"Well, then, J.W., the oldest case will be heard first. If a 'dinner adjournment' is not convenient, none will be taken. I would suggest you come with me for a little refreshment. It could be a long day."

As we walked down to the hotel, Judge Wheeler stepped up by my side.

"Will, you might want to think about not adjourning for dinner. This could cause some problems with some of the attorney's appearing before your court."

"My court?"

"Of course."

"Then if some of those round bellied gentlemen are upset, maybe they'd better try another court."

"But, Will, there is no other court, short of Appellate."

"Ain't that a fact."

Taking me and Thomas Wagner by the arm he pulled us into a door way.

"Judge Jackson," he began, "I don't know how to say this, and frankly, I never thought I'd have to. But, my friend, you must not let your new positions power overturn your good judgement. You must live, and work with these attorneys. They can make your life very difficult if you try to ride rough shod over them."

"He's right, Will. Sometimes it is best to walk softly at first."

"Gentlemen, I would be hard put to even measure my debt of gratitude to both of you. And, please don't misunderstand my motives. I am not puffed up with my new job. But, please, understand where I'm coming from. I see the duties of this job to be only to the people, and after that to the officers of my court, including myself. It's not my intent to smuggle a sandwich to cover my hunger or to allow any other to do so. But, I've seen lawyers do their clients an injustice by the breaks and postponements they take in a case. Did you get a glance at the docket Mr. Fisher had? There were at least eighteen or twenty cases. And, I'm sure some of those people have waited long for their day in court. Gentlemen, for most of my life, my work day has begun with the sun and ended with its absence. I see no reason to change. Anyone who intends to ride the river with me had better be ready to start, and quit, when I do."

"Just be careful, Will, try not to go too fast," Judge Wheeler advised.

We all went on to the hotel, after my talk with two of my advisors.

Not much was said or settled in my mind during this respite from the days activities. After about half an hour, I called an end to the gathering by announcing my return to court.

J.W. Fisher and I led the group back to the court house. Again I felt I was in the way of making a grand fool of myself.

Chapter 4

I told Fisher to advise the sheriff to bring the accused murderer to the courtroom and for the sheriff to round up the witnesses for the trial. I told J.W. to tell the sheriff he had thirty minutes to get it done. J.W. just looked at me, then shaking his head went straight away toward the sheriffs office.

When I entered the courtroom, it was still filled with people standing around as if waiting for the show to begin.

I turned to Judge Wheeler.

"Judge, is it customary for a circuit judge to wear some kind of robe or anything like that?"

"I do in Denver, but, as you know, Thomas sits in a business suit. It's pretty much up to you."

"Good! I would feel even more the fool to have to wear such before these people."

"There is one thing, Will," Jamie said stepping around Judge Wheeler. "You will always need a gavel. I had one made and the brass band is engraved with your name and today's date." With that, he handed me a real good-looking gavel with a two inch engraved brass band around its head.

"How in the world could you have had this done so fast. I've known for less than a week if I would accept this job!"

"Oh, shoot, Will, I've known for two weeks that there would be a day soon when you'd need the gavel. I had only the date to be inscribed at the last moment. The gavel I had made two weeks ago. Everyone who knows you, knew the day would come. It's not our fault it took you so long to find out what we've all known for some time."

I looked around me to see sly smiles and grins on the faces of all I knew.

I said no more. Just took the proffered gavel, tapped Jamie on the shoulder and stepped around to the bench.

My first act as a judge was to clear the courtroom of all except lawyers, judges and law enforcement. The dirtiest look I got, for the order, was from my own Uncle Buck.

When spectators were gone, I sat, and advised those who remained to do likewise.

"Gentlemen," I began after all were seated, "few of you know anything at all about me. I am told there are a few local attorneys' present and the rest are either travelers with me and my court, or are here to see if the new judge can find his way to his own chair."

In response to this remark was an array of laughs, smiles, grins and even some stone faces.

"Well, let us understand one another. I suspect there are a few in this room who have the power to have me removed from this bench. I suspect there are some who in the future might even try, whether or not they have the power to get the job done."

"Now, listen carefully to what I say next because I'll not ever say it again. I will run this court as honestly as I can. I will not tolerate lazy lawyers or lack of preparation on the part of any attorney who appears in this court. It matters not which side you may represent. And, fellows, that about says it all. Be honest, be prepared and don't try to pull anything funny on me, or those poor souls, who, for whatever reason find themselves a foul of the law. Oh, and one additional thing; I had me a right good job when they came and offered me this one. Should I for any reason lose this one, I can go back to what I left. And boys the one I had paid better than this one!"

Even some of the stone faces grinned at the last remark.

I then turned to J.W. "Mr. Fisher, you may readmit the spectators, and then call the first case."

"Your honor!" shouted one of the attorneys. "Given the hour, might it not be appropriate to adjourn for lunch?"

"Counselor, if you mean, shouldn't we all go out and have an early dinner, the answer is no. Mr. Fisher, if you please."

That started quite a grumbling.

J.W. readmitted the crowd and after the sheriff had brought in a scruffy looking older man and sat him at one of the tables facing my desk, J.W. called the first case as the Territory versus Jack O'Connor; on the charge of murder.

"Is the defense ready?" I asked.

"Yes, sir," said an older gentleman arising from the first row behind the rail. I remembered him as one of the stone faces.

"Prosecution?"

"Your honor," said the one who had wanted an early 'lunch', may I approach!"

"Will defense council join us?" I asked.

Both attorneys came forward to stand in front of me.

"Sir," began the hungry one, "my name is Wilton Mayhugh. I was appointed by Judge Claus to prosecute Mr. O'Connor, when last the Judge held court here."

"Fine Mr. Mayhugh, and when was that?" I asked.

"In June of this year, sir."

"Three months ago?"

"I believe that's right, sir."

"And you, sir?" I asked turning to the defense council.

"Abel Tyson, sir," was the curt response.

"So, Mr. Mayhugh, what's your problem?"

"Sir, due to unforseen circumstances, I am forced to request a continuance to better prepare for the prosecution of Mr. O'Connor."

"Have you been ill, Mr. Mayhugh?"

"No, sir."

"Has a member of your family been seriously ill?"

"No, sir."

I turned to Mr. Tyson. "And you, sir, are you ready with the defense?"

"We are, your honor."

"Mr. Mayhugh, do you not feel you can prosecute this case, at this time."

"Well, your honor, I could do so much better with a postponement."

"Sheriff," I said, "what is your name sir?"

"Dom Cribari, sir."

"Have you many witnesses against Mr. O'Connor?"

"No, sir. Only one."

"And that witness sir, did he see Mr. O'Connor do the murder in question?"

"No, sir, he says he only heard Mr. O'Connor saying how glad he was the deceased had been killed."

"Mr. Cribari, has your office found any physical evidence Mr. O'Connor committed the crime with which he is charged?"

"We found a .45 Colt at Mr. O'Connor's cabin, that had recently been fired."

"Mr. Cribari, I hope you won't hold it against me, but I have a .45 Colt in my grip over at the hotel and I must confess, it, also has recently been fired. I shot a wolf on the way down here," I said.

"No, your honor."

"Very well, sir, have you any other evidence against Mr. O'Connor?"

"No sir."

"Mr. Mayhugh, have you any other evidence against Mr. O'Connor?"

"No sir, but I'm sure if you will only allow me a postponement, I can present a strong case against the accused."

"Mr. Mayhugh, you have had three months and have failed to prepare yourself to present any case at all. Step back gentlemen."

When the men had returned to their tables, I looked around the courtroom.

"Well, big shot," I thought, "here goes. Now we're going to see some fireworks."

"Mr. O'Connor, please stand," I said.

O'Connor and Tyson both stood.

"Mr. O'Connor, the charges against you are dismissed, and just so there'll be nothing brought up in the future I am directing my clerk to have the record show that I am directing a verdict of 'not guilty' be entered upon your behalf. I am sure your attorney can explain the 'double jeopardy' point of law to you."

Tyson smiled and O'Connor raised his head for the first time since coming into the courtroom.

"Now, Mr. Cribari, if you please, remove the chains from Mr. O'Connor. He is a free man. And, also, Mr. Cribari, who directed you to arrest and hold Mr. O'Connor?"

"Mr. Mayhugh did, sir. He said Judge Claus told him to do so."

"Very well, sir." I then turned my attention to Mayhugh.

"Well, Mr. Mayhugh, so that you are perfectly clear as to what I will demand of those who serve as officers of my court; I find you in contempt and fine you one hundred dollars. Sir, obviously my little talk earlier on made no impression upon you. Possibly this citation will bring home my point and the way I will run my court. We have one purpose in our jobs here, and that is to serve the people of this territory in a competent and timely manner. And, sir, that means all the people, the innocent, the accused, and the guilty. Those whom we serve have not only an expectation of prompt and speedy service by us, the officers of this court, they have a constitutional guarantee of such promptness. I assume you have read the Constitution, Mr. Mayhugh? I will demand the same timeliness of those officers of this court, as I intend to afford those who appear before it. Your failure to pay this fine immediately will result in your serving thirty days in the county jail!"

"You can't do that!" Mayhugh said, standing there pounding on his table with his fist.

I waited until he and the courtroom had settled down.

"Mr. Mayhugh," I said quietly, "would you care to try for two hundred dollars or sixty days?"

You could have heard a pin drop in the courtroom.

"I don't have a hundred dollars on me. I'd have to go to the bank," Mayhugh finally muttered.

"You have thirty minutes to do so. Mr. Fisher, may we have the next case."

The rest of the day was more interesting to the spectators and attorneys than to me. While I did not adjourn for lunch, I noticed only two people leaving at noon. The rest of the four cases I heard that day were minor civil cases. Two were uncontested debt collection cases, one a suit to establish parentage for an illegitimate child and the final a case over damages done to a business by a drunk miner. None of them were too serious, and in each the attorneys presented themselves as well prepared and quite respectful.

At four-thirty, and the end of the last case, I obtained the docket and announced the cases I would hear the next day. I was a tad ambitious in the number of cases I scheduled. I told those present that should a case end at or about noon, we would recess for dinner. But those involved should come prepared, if such was not the case. I further warned all present that my courtroom was not a café, and I would not tolerate eating or drinking therein.

When the room had cleared except for my family, the judges, and J.W., I looked over at Judge Wheeler.

"Sir, did I go too far?" I asked.

"Let me just say, Will, you did today what I have often wanted to do, but had not the personal courage to follow through."

"Was what I did really legal?"

"You asked earlier, 'is it your court?' As for the legality: to hold one in contempt of your court is pretty much a judgment call. While the penalty might have been a little harsh, that, also, is your call. All in all, I'd say you had a good day. At least those here today have little doubt as to your sincerity."

"As for me, Will, I was proud of you and felt truly rewarded for the small time I spent with you," said Thomas Wagner.

"Will, just let me toss in my two-bits worth," spoke up Jamie Nava. "What you did was right and just. As for all the rest, don't worry. If what you do is always as right as what you did today, you will never have to back up for your pay!"

"Hear, hear!" said Judge Wheeler.

"Now folks," I said, "speaking of pay, I intend to reward you all with the finest dinner that the hotel can put on. It's my turn to give back a little of the good wishes you folks have showered on me!"

"Judge Jackson," Ralph Wheeler began, "it was my intent to catch a train back to Denver at seven this evening, but frankly this is one celebration I wouldn't miss if I have to go home horseback."

"Will, you have arrived!" Thomas Wagner exclaimed.

Startled, I looked at him, "How's that, sir?"

"Simply, that Ralph Wheeler hates nothing in this world more than riding a horse. For him to even mention such in passing, is quite a statement, indeed! And, what's more, let's drop this 'sir' and 'judge.' I think we will all feel more comfortable with first names."

"I heartedly endorse that," Ralph said.

"J.W.," I said, turning to my clerk, "is your family here or elsewhere?"

"I have no family, sir."

"Well, then, you get cleaned up here, then will you please join us in the hotel dining room at seven. That'll give everyone time to wash up for supper." I turned to face my group. "Is that all right?"

All agreed and we trooped from the courtroom. I was no less concerned about my ability to function well in my new job, but at least the lines had been drawn. One thing I'd decided on the trip from our ranch to Trinidad was that if I was going to do this thing, it would be in absolute keeping with my beliefs. I had no intent to foist my personal faith upon my court but I've worked hard all my life. When it is time to work, I'd always been there. When I completed a job, I could say I'd done my best. My court would operate that way or I'd have no court. Upon that I'd brook no compromise.

Chapter 5

Clatilda and I sat in our room that first evening after receiving my commission as a judge; she brushing her hair and I was going over the cases I was to hear the next day.

"Will. Would you mind if I sent the family on home and the twins, Jacob and I stay here with you for a while?"

"Of course not. After I leave here, I have two days in Alamosa, then J.W. says I have two weeks before I have to be in Durango. We could have supper with Jamie and his daughter in Alamosa before we go home together."

"Can I plan on that?"

"Sure, what's the problem. And, also, why do you want Jacob to stay here?"

"Will, I'm concerned. Jacob and I heard some men talking in the lobby. They said you'd be 'straightened out' before you left Trinidad."

"Who were these men, and where did you hear them talking?"

"I don't know them, Will, and we heard them in the lobby just before we went into the dining room for supper."

"What you probably heard were some lawyers, upset by my actions. They are probably cooking up some way to try to embarrass me in court."

"Be that, as it may, will it still be all right if Jacob stays with me and the twins?"

"Ma'am, are you really that upset?"

"Just cautious, cowboy. I think you can take care of what you see coming. I just want Jacob to watch your back."

"You are frightened?"

"Some."

"Jacob stays. Maybe you should get him to loan you one of his arsenal of pistols he carries."

"I don't need one."

I looked sharply at her to see that she was not teasing me.

"You have a weapon?"

"I do."

"Is it loaded?"

"I checked."

"Derringer?"

"Silver and shiny."

"Well, keep it in your purse. I wouldn't want the judge's wife seen carrying around a cannon."

"Will, are you aware Jacob carries three or four pistols?"

"I'm only aware that I asked him to thin down his arsenal before we came down here. If he's still carrying that many guns, I hesitate to think what he carried before."

When we walked over to the courthouse, the next morning, I was surprised to find the courtroom mostly full. I had expected a much smaller crowd.

Uncle Buck, Bud and the Blalocks had left for home right after an early breakfast. Uncle Buck and Bud grumbling that they had to go home.

J.W. was at my bench when I walked into the courtroom. He told me he had the first three cases ready and had told the sheriff to arrange to get the parties for the fourth and fifth cases ready as soon as the second case was over.

I looked at this little man. He looked me right in the eye.

"You'll do, J.W., you'll do," I said putting my hand on his shoulder as I stepped around him to my chair.

The first case was a simple case of theft and, as the evidence was overwhelming, was disposed of quickly.

The second case involved two persons, both claiming ownership of a piece of ground, halfway up Raton Pass.

As I was looking over the two complaints, I was interrupted.

"If it please the court?" spoke one of the attorneys.

I looked up to see Wilton Mayhugh again standing before my bench.

"Yes, counselor," I answered.

"We wish to petition for a change of venue, sir."

"On what grounds, sir?" I asked.

"We feel we cannot receive a fair hearing, on this matter, in this court."

Mr. Mayhugh now had my full attention.

"Which of the complainants do you represent, Mr. Mayhugh?"

"I speak for both, sir."

"Whoa. Let's back up some. Where's the other attorney? I'm sure you don't presume to speak for both sides of this issue."

"I have been asked by Jack Palmer, the attorney representing Mr. Genoa to present this request for both parties."

"And where, may I ask, is Mr. Palmer?"

"He is indisposed this morning, sir."

I listened as a buzz and some quiet laughter went through the spectators.

Somehow I was made very uneasy by this.

"Mr. Mayhugh, do you, by any chance, know the nature of Mr. Palmer's distress?"

"Not really, sir. I believe it has to do with a stomach ailment."

This statement brought forth some loud laughter.

I sat for a moment, while the courtroom quieted down.

"Mr. Cribari," I said, turning to the sheriff, "do you know where Mr. Palmer lives?"

"Yes, your honor. He's staying at the same hotel you're in. He travels with your court."

"Then this court will take a fifteen minute recess while you determine the seriousness of Mr. Palmer's health problems. If there is any assistance this court may offer him, assure Mr. Palmer we are at his service."

As the sheriff started out of the courtroom, Mayhugh made as if to follow.

"Mr. Mayhugh, a moment of your time, sir!" I said.

"But, sir, I'm going to see if I can help the sheriff."

"This will only take a moment," I said standing at my bench.

A plainly disgusted Mayhugh turned and stepped up to the bench.

Making no effort to quieten or disguise my tone, I looked down at Mayhugh.

"Counselor, I don't yet know exactly what's going on. But be aware, sir, I will. If there are any shenanigans going on concerning Mr. Palmer's absence or this motion for a venue change, hell won't hold what will rain down on the people involved. Do I make myself clear, sir?"

"Your new position in this courtroom gives you no such authority to speak to me like that, sir!"

"Mr. Mayhugh, I don't know what, if any, god you worship. But, whoever He is, you'd be well advised to offer a prayer to him that any problems you and I have stay in this courtroom. Because, sir, I believe you would not be pleased with the outcome, should our differences spill out into the street."

"This from a so-called leader in his religious community!" said Mr. Mayhugh, taking a step back.

I felt myself losing control of my temper and quickly seated myself.

"Please return to your chair, Mr. Mayhugh. We may or may not continue this discussion, but nothing will happen now."

It was only moments before Sheriff Cribari returned to the courtroom. Approaching the bench, he spoke quietly, almost in a whisper.

"Judge Jackson, may we speak privately?" he asked.

"Of course," I said.

"Judge," Cribari said, leaning over the bench, "Mr. Palmer will be here in just a few minutes."

"Does he feel like it? I supposed him to be really sick."

"No, sir, I wouldn't say 'really sick'—really hung-over is more like it. And in pretty bad shape, I'd say."

"Is he coming to court anyway?"

"Yes, sir, he said he'd be here within a half hour, and that's been almost ten minutes ago, now," Cribari said, looking at his watch.

I banged my gavel and called for order.

"This court will continue in recess until Mr. Palmer gets here, which should be within the next twenty minutes. All except those involved in the current proceedings may leave the courtroom. Providing, if upon your return you find court in session, you return to your seats quietly."

Once again I sat back in my chair and thought about the past day and a half. I knew I had already created one sure enemy and possibly many more. This was not the type of failure I had anticipated, but failure, it surely was. I wondered at myself. Was I so sure of myself that I should lay down such hard and fast rules in an area I had only just entered? Had I, indeed, became so puffed up with my own importance that I had to be the boss regardless of the feelings of others? Oh, how I wished for a few moments with my Clatilda. More, even a few moments by myself, that I might pray for guidance.

"Well, stupid," I thought. "You're not doing anything real important, right now. What better time to pray."

I leaned back in my chair and covered my eyes with one hand. When I took my problem to the Lord, I somehow expected the type of answer, I'd received twice before. But no such answer was forthcoming. I prayed for a while longer before I sensed a quietness in the room. I sat forward, taking my hand from my eyes.

The first thing I saw was Clatilda intently looking at me with her fist clenched beside her face. This had long been our signal, one to the other, to hold fast.

I then glanced over to see a sad sight, indeed. Standing beside one of the tables was a young man who appeared to be at death's door. He trembled sheepishly as he stood there, his face was white as a sheet and the circles around his eyes could have been painted there with charcoal.

"Mr. Palmer, I assume?" I asked.

"Yes, your honor, and may I apologize to the court for my tardiness."

"Do you feel well enough to continue, sir?" I asked.

"Yes, your honor, I do wish to do so."

"Very well, sir, there is a motion before the court for a change of venue, placed there by Mr. Mayhugh, your opposing counsel. He stated to the court he spoke for you both in this matter. Is this true?"

"No, sir, it is not, and I can't believe Mr. Mayhugh would have said it was!"

"You advised me to do so last night," Mayhugh said, jumping to his feet.

"You will both approach!" I said.

When they were standing just in front of me, I leaned forward slightly putting my face no more than eighteen inches from theirs.

"Now, my friends, I will know, and right now, just exactly what's going on here!"

"I don't know, sir, but I never thought to request a change of venue. Mayhugh suggested it last night but I disagreed," said Palmer.

"How would you remember what you agreed to? You were so drunk. You had to be carried to your room!"

"As drunk as I was, there is no way I would have agreed to anything as stupid as a motion for change of venue!"

"That's enough!" I said. "Step back, gentlemen."

They returned to their tables.

"There will be a ten minute recess," I announced. "But first, is Mr. Tyson in the courtroom?"

"I am, your honor," Tyson said, standing up from a chair in the front corner of the room.

"Sir, would you be kind enough to meet me in the sheriff's office?"

"As you wish, sir."

Followed by Tyson and led by the sheriff, I quickly made my way down the hall to the sheriff's office.

"Have you a room where Mr. Tyson and I can meet privately, sheriff?" I asked as we entered a large complex consisting of even a jail cell in its rear.

"Yes, sir. You may use my office," answered Sheriff Cribari.

We went into his office, and I closed the door behind me.

"Mr. Tyson, I have but two questions of you and will not keep you long."

"Please be advised, sir, I will not be singled out, to discuss others in the cadre of attorneys who follow your court."

"Nor would I put anyone in such a position. As I said, I have only two questions, sir. The first is, do you often drink to excess?"

Tyson stood for a moment, looking me directly in the eye.

"Not that it is any of your business, sir, but I occasionally have a glass of wine at dinner. If one is to be had. Beyond that, I find alcohol distasteful."

"Secondly, have you ever seen Mr. Palmer appear in court in the condition he's in this morning?"

"Never!"

"Thank you, Mr. Tyson. Now let's return to the courtroom."

"If you don't mind, sir, I need to talk to a client of mine who, now, is a guest of Sheriff Cribari."

"Very well, sir."

I returned to the court and called it to order.

"Now, Mr. Mayhugh, in response to your motion for a change of venue, I will now hear your arguments supporting this motion."

Mayhugh sat at his table for a long moment staring down.

"Your honor, it is obvious, after your actions yesterday, that any client I represent in your court would not receive a fair hearing. Given that the nature of this suit represents my client's entire personal worth, I believe he must be provided the fairest possible arena for his case."

"Very well, sir. Mr. Palmer have you anything to say?"

"Only that to change the venue of this matter would require both petitioners, Mr. Mayhugh and myself, to travel at least to Pueblo, and frankly, sir, my client cannot afford to pay me to do so, let alone provide for his own travel expenses."

I noticed Mayhugh's client grab Mayhugh's arm and engage in a quiet, but very earnest discussion. Mayhugh kept shaking his head and tried to quieten his client.

Finally the man stood, pushing back his chair.

"Judge, my name's Sam Prather. Can I ask you a question?"

"What is your question, sir?"

"If we change this venue thing, will a new judge come here or will we have to go somewhere else to get this thing straightened out?"

"Mr. Prather, if I permit a change of venue, you will have to go to another court. In all probability, that other court will be in Pueblo."

Prather looked down at Mayhugh with a look, not of respect.

Loud enough to be heard all over the silent courtroom, "You lied to me, Mayhugh! You said another judge would come down here. You said that other fellow didn't know what he was talking about. You lied!"

I sat, wondering what part I should, or even could, take in the matter.

Prather and Mayhugh solved my dilemma.

"I've seen some folks get fired in the mines for lying about what they'd done. I guess that's what I'm gonna do to you, Mayhugh. You're fired!" Prather said.

"You can't do that, Sam! Sit down and shut up!"

I banged my gavel on the bench.

"Oh yes, Mr. Prather! You can do that. With my permission."

"Well, Judge, I'd sure like to fire this man, and I can't afford to go to Pueblo. I can't even hardly afford no lawyer, anyhow. All I want is to just stay in my home and not be bothered."

"Mr. Mayhugh, had you prepared to present Mr. Prather's case, in the event you were to have been his attorney, and the case was to have been tried in my court?"

"Well, sir, I had only a few loose ends. Then, yes, I would be ready."

"Mr. Palmer, are you ready to go to trial?"

"Yes, your honor."

"Very well, then, Mr. Prather you have until 1:00 P.M. tomorrow to hire another attorney. Mr. Mayhugh will turn his files over to your new attorney."

"What about my fee?" demanded Mayhugh.

"Considering, this court neither hired you nor fired you, do not look to it for your fee."

"Next case," I demanded of J.W.

The rest of that day was without consequences, but Clatilda, the twins, Jacob and I had barely seated ourselves at the supper table in the hotel that evening when we were interrupted by Jack Palmer.

"Judge Jackson, I hate to interrupt your dinner, but, sir, I must speak to you privately."

We went out on the hotel's porch and sat ourselves at the end away from others.

"Now, Mr. Palmer, what's so important that it couldn't wait until morning?"

"Sir, I just came from a meeting with C. R. Clinton, a local attorney. He is Mr. Prather's new attorney. He says Mr. Mayhugh refuses to release the Prather file to him. He says Mayhugh will not do so until Prather settles his fee."

"Mr. Palmer, I believe Mr. Mayhugh is within his rights to take that position."

"What are we to do, sir? You have set a trial time that cannot be met by Mr. Clinton, without the case file."

"Mr. Palmer, I am a judge, not some school teacher. I will not play the guardian of a bunch of children in some school yard fight. There are matters over which I'll not assume control. You three settle your disputes or come to me with a problem my court has the authority to settle. I'll not advise, dictate, or even suggest what you should do to settle this matter."

Palmer left me, and I returned to my supper. Jacob and Clatilda acted as if nothing had happened.

Later that evening in our room, Clatilda asked if Mr. Palmer had upset me.

"Ma'am, I don't know if this is the job for me. Nothing about it seems to my liking. This sparring back and forth like a bunch of kids is not my way. I surely believe that one of these days I'll come down from behind my bench and settle one of these squabbles, in a more straightforward and physical way than the law will allow."

"Will, do you want to resign your commission and return to the ranch?"

"Almost more than anything I have ever wanted to do in my life."

"Do you think you have given it a fair enough test to make that decision?"

"I don't know, Clatilda, I just don't know. I only know that if the past two days represent what I can expect as a judge, I want no part of it."

"Will, have you thought of talking over the situation with Mr. Fisher?"

"My clerk?"

"Yes, Will. He was with Judge Claus for ten years, according to what he said at supper last night. Surely he can tell you what you can expect."

"You know, you may be right. He's here in this hotel. I'll go see him now."

"What if he's already asleep?"

"Then I'll wake him."

He was, and I did.

"What can I do for you, Judge?" A very sleepy J.W. Fisher asked, standing at his door in only his britches with one gallus over his shoulder, the other drooping at his side.

"J.W., you can start by excusing me for awakening you. Then you can give me permission to come in and talk to you."

"Of course, sir. Please do come in. Excuse me while I properly dress myself."

"Put on a shirt if you like, J.W. If not, just sit down. I don't ever intend you and I to be so formal that we need coats and ties just to have a talk."

He looked at me for a moment, then hitched his other gallus over his shoulder and motioned me to a small table sitting in one corner of his room.

We sat, he slightly less comfortably than I.

"J.W., I understand you were with Judge Claus for a number of years?"

"Yes sir. Ten years and two months at the time of his death."

"Then, partner, I've got a bunch of questions for you."

"I hope I can be of help, sir."

"J.W., was Judge Claus' court ever so fouled up as mine has been the past two days?"

"No, sir."

I sat there, for a moment, looking at this man, who returned my gaze, unflinchingly.

"Just that? No, sir?"

"I believe I answered your question, sir."

"All right, J.W., let's get a couple of things square, right off. First, when it's just you and me, you will please call me by my first name. And, secondly, when I ask you a question, I would much appreciate not only the facts but also your opinion and comments. Can you handle that?"

"Firstly, sir, it was not the custom between Judge Claus and me to deal with one another with familiarity. And secondly, I've always felt it better to keep my personal opinions to myself."

"J.W., you mean you've never had anyone you could talk openly with?"

"No, sir. As you know, I am not married. Nor, have I ever been. I worked for a judge in Ohio before coming west for my health. So, I've always had to keep my own counsel, and just never found anyone with whom I could talk freely."

"J.W., what do you intend doing in the two weeks we have off after our stint in Alamosa?"

"I thought to go on to Durango. There, to await your arrival."

"You ever been on a working ranch?"

"No, sir."

"Then, you're not going to Durango, you're coming home with me."

"Oh, I'm afraid I couldn't do that, sir."

"Why not?"

"It wouldn't be proper."

"Proper!"

"No, sir. I am in your employ, and as such, I would not be comfortable as a guest in your home."

"Have you met my friend, Jacob Webber?"

"Yes, sir, last evening."

"He, also, is in my employ."

"But I thought him to be your friend."

"He is that, also. But there was a time he started to steal my cattle, and might even have killed me."

"And you call this man your friend?"

"Yes, J.W., one of my best! Now, first, will you come to the ranch?"

"If you insist, sir."

"Then will you call me by my first name, when we're outside the court?"

"That will take some effort, sir."

"Will you try?"

"Yes, sir— uh, Will."

"There, now let's get back to the reason I came down here. Was Judge Claus' court ever so rowdy as mine?"

"No, sir."

"Because?"

"Well, sir, I would say it was mainly because Judge Claus was not quite the disciplinarian you seem to be."

"Please explain."

"Well, sir, Judge Claus was more inclined to want as little disruption of his day as possible."

"All right, but how would he have dealt with Mr. Mayhugh's request for a continuance yesterday?"

"He would have granted it, sir."

"When would he have heard the case then?"

"The next time he was in Trinidad."

"Could that be why you have so many cases on the docket?"

"Eight of those cases were held over from the last time Judge Claus sat here, in Trinidad."

"Including, possibly, the O'Connor murder case?"

"Including the O'Connor murder case."

"That phony shyster!"

"I must say, I was pleased by that little piece of business with Mayhugh yesterday."

"J.W., what do you think I can look forward to in the future? More like the past two days or might things level out a bit?"

"By and large, sir, you seem to have identified your worst adversary. The attorneys who travel with your court were all here the past two days and are generally a quieter, more professional group."

"Does Mayhugh travel with the court, or is he a local product?"

"He has been following this court for the past four years."

"Do you know where he came from?"

"It is my understanding, sir, he came from Missouri."

"J.W., if I get in trouble, who comes to chew me out, and who can fire me?"

"I am not sure, sir. I know there was once a problem in Judge Claus' court and Judge Wheeler from Denver came down. He said he was sent by the governor."

"Judge Ralph Wheeler?"

"Yes, sir."

"Well, at least I'll get a fair hearing."

"Do you anticipate trouble, Judge Jackson?"

"J.W., I always expect trouble. I work on the theory that I'll trust most folks, but I'll always cut the cards."

"That brings up another subject, sir. Do you play poker?"

"Why, no I don't, J.W. Why do you ask?"

"Well, sir, as I said, the gentlemen who travel with your court are generally professional, but they play a particularly vicious game of poker. Why, sir, last year, in Pagosa Springs, Mr. Tyson and Mr. Gentry actually got into a fist fight over an extra ace in the deck."

"Our Mr. Tyson?"

"Yes sir, and Mr. Gentry gave him the worst black eye I've ever seen!"

"Well, I'll be!" I said. "Those are two fellows I'm just rightly going to have to get to know better."

"I hope not to play poker with them, sir."

"No, J.W., absolutely not to play poker with them. J.W., I see you taking a lot of notes during court. Just how much do you get?"

"All of it, sir."

"Surely not every word, and who said it?"

"Sir, on two different occasions my notes have gone to the Supreme Court of these United States. And on neither occasion were they even questioned, let alone disputed."

"Sir," I said, "I am surely impressed! I thought to stand in awe of some of the more experienced attorneys. I'd no idea my own clerk would out shine us all!"

"Oh, Judge, it was not so much."

"Nevertheless, Mr. Fisher, I think there will be no more silly talk of my firing you. You must have gotten quite a laugh out of my bluster!"

"Sir, what you asked of Judge Wheeler were perfectly logical questions. On the contrary, sir, I was impressed with your forthright attitude."

"J.W., it will be my pleasure to have you at my home next month as a friend, not an employee."

That bald-headed little sucker smiled from ear to ear.

"J.W., I think I've settled on a plan for tomorrow. It will either rid us of Mayhugh, or this court of me. Either way, things are going to change, beginning at 1 o'clock tomorrow."

"May I know of your plan, sir?"

"No, J.W., and not because I don't trust you. It's just that I've a few kinks I have yet to work out. Just keep your pen sharp tomorrow. There may be a need for very accurate and complete notes."

I then said good night and went back to my room. Clatilda had put the twins down but she was still awake.

"Did you have a good meeting with Mr. Fisher?" she said as I walked in.

"Yeah, I did. What's more I learned a couple of things about our Mr. Fisher. Do you know that little old guy has had his court notes figure in two cases heard before the Supreme Court?"

"Of the United States?"

"Of the United States!"

"This was the clerk you wanted to know if you could fire if he didn't work out?"

"Yeah, there's no question about it, is there? When I set out to make a fool of myself, I generally do a bang-up job, don't I?"

"I'll say one thing, Will. I am very pleased you have such a competent man working with you. Was he able to help you?"

"Yes, he was. It seems Mayhugh is the only real bad apple in the barrel. The rest of the attorneys who appear in my court are generally, according to J.W., professional in their attitudes."

"Do you trust Mr. Fisher's opinion?"

"Yes, ma'am, I do. I'd be hard put to tell you exactly why but, yes, I do."

"Have you decided what you are going to do?"

"Not completely, but I've just about figured it out. At least by two, tomorrow afternoon, I figure it will all be over, but for the shouting!"

"Will, have you prayed about it?"

"Not yet, but I will tonight."

And pray I did. Not so much for any striking revelation, but rather that I might have the strength and wisdom to handle the next day in an honest, straightforward manner. I dared not hope, or even pray, for Solomon-like wisdom, just for presence of mind enough not to make a fool of myself.

Chapter 6

The morning of the third day of my new job dawned cloudy and overcast, with a threat of snow. A perfect match for my mood.

I had slept well but awakened with the thought of the days portent, a leaden weight on my mind.

Jacob and Clatilda sensed my shadowy mood at breakfast and little was said except by the twins. Jessie insisting she had seen a few snowflakes through the front window of the hotel when we came down into the lobby. Jake argued she was wrong. It was sort of nice to see children acting like children instead of grown men acting as the same children. Clatilda tried to shush them but I insisted she allow them to be themselves. This helped greatly in lightening my temper.

Clatilda had arranged for the wife of the day desk clerk to care for the twins that day. When she had done so, I didn't know, but I was relieved they should not witness what might go on in the courtroom that day.

The morning dragged by as a fingernail being scraped down a school room blackboard, irritating and endless.

As it happened, the last case that morning ended right at noon. I recessed the court until one that afternoon.

Dinner was a blur, and it seemed only a few short minutes until I was back in the courtroom rapping my gavel for order.

"Mr. Fisher, if you please, may we have the next case?"

J.W. stood and called the case of Fuller *vs.* Prather.

Jack Palmer stood and Mr. Prather did likewise.

"Judge Jackson," Prather began, "I have no lawyer to represent me. I had promised to pay Mr. Mayhugh's fee over the next three months. But he won't give my case files to Mr. Clinton unless I pay the entire fee now. Mr. Clinton says he can't be my lawyer until and unless he can go over my case file. Sir, I haven't been able to live in my house since this thing came to court. This summer that's not been too much of a problem, but with the weather turning as it is, I need a solid shelter."

"Is Mr. Clinton in the courtroom?" I asked.

A tall, grey-haired, man stood and identified himself as C. R. Clinton.

"Sir, have you asked Mr. Mayhugh for Mr. Prather's file?"

"Yes, sir. And he says he will not release it until his fee is paid. And, sir, I can't say I blame him."

"Thank you, Mr. Clinton," I said. "Is Wilton Mayhugh in the courtroom?"

"I sure am!" Mayhugh said, standing just outside the rail separating the court and spectators.

"Mr. Mayhugh, have you Mr. Prather's file?"

"I have, and I am within my rights not releasing it until my fee is paid."

"I agree, Mr. Mayhugh. Did you make an agreement with Mr. Prather to pay your fee over the three months following this hearing?"

"Yes, but that was when I was his attorney. You allowed him to end that relationship yesterday!"

"Mr. Prather, I told you yesterday the court would allow you to discharge your attorney. But today you tell me you have no attorney. Is that a fact?"

"That's right, Judge."

"Mr. Prather, it is usually the litigant's choice for their case to be decided by a jury or by the judge. Do you understand?"

"If you mean by litigants, me and Fuller; then yes, I'd be willing to let you decide. As for Fuller, you'd have to ask him."

"Mr. Palmer, your client's wish: trial by jury or a decision by the court?"

Palmer turned and spoke briefly with the man by his side.

"We, as Mr. Prather, would be perfectly satisfied to have this case adjudicated by your honor."

"Does that mean you will decide?" Prather pressed.

"Yes, Mr. Prather, that's exactly what it means. Now, Mr. Prather, I told you, yesterday you could discharge your attorney. But I am afraid, sir, I cannot allow such a complicated case as yours to be tried without your having legal representation. I am, therefore, rescinding my order of yesterday and reinstating Mr. Mayhugh as your attorney."

Two men shouted, almost as one, "You can't do that!" Mayhugh and Prather.

"Oh, but yes, gentlemen, I can, and I am. Mr. Palmer, are you ready, sir?"

"Yes, your honor," Palmer stated simply, but he could not completely hide his small grin.

"Mr. Mayhugh, are you ready?"

"You've gone too far, this time, Jackson. I'll see you off the bench for this."

"Normally, I would address you more privately than I am about to, but this time I will make an exception! Sir, if and when you ever address this bench again, you will do so by prefacing your remarks with 'Judge Jackson' or 'your honor.' Should you fail to do so, sir, I will take it as a personal insult and not as an insult to the court. And, sir, I settle my personal problems personally. I spent almost my entire life as a working cowhand. How have you spent your's, sir?"

I sat and allowed my remarks to sink in on Mayhugh for a slow count of ten.

"Now, Mr. Mayhugh, I would suggest you step to the table, beside your client and answer my question. Are you ready to begin this trial, counselor?"

Mayhugh slowly stepped through the gate and up to Prather's table. Laying his satchel on the table, he turned slowly and faced me.

"Judge Jackson," he began, now looking at the floor, "I am not completely prepared. If you will allow this case to be heard the day after tomorrow, I will be prepared to successfully present Mr. Prather's case."

I sat for a moment, stunned by what I had fully expected. It took a moment for me to gather my wits about me.

"Gentlemen, I am sure there is an attorney in this courtroom that would be willing and capable to handle Mr. Prather's case, pro bono. Will that gentleman please raise his hand?"

Four hands jumped up, scattered throughout the room.

"Will you four gentlemen please confer among yourselves, and one of you meet with Mr. Prather this afternoon to prepare yourselves for the trial of this matter, Friday at three P.M."

Turning back to Mayhugh, I stared at him for a moment while I silently offered a sincere prayer for what I was about to do.

"Mr. Mayhugh, it is the direction of this court that you immediately surrender Mr. Prather's case file to the clerk. Sir, you will surrender it in its entirety. Failure to do so will result in more dire results than you may think possible."

Taking a deep breath, I leaned forward, resting my elbows on the bench and looking directly into Mayhugh's eyes.

"And, furthermore, sir, you are never again to present yourself as an officer of this court. Whatever cases you may have pending in this court's jurisdiction, you can either arrange other representation for your clients or this court shall. In more direct language sir, I never wish to see you again, with the possible exception of as a defendant in a criminal case."

Mayhugh now stood stock still, his face white as a sheet.

"This time, Judge, you've gone too far. You haven't the authority to keep me from my profession, from practicing law! Only the governor can do that."

"It is not my intent, sir, to keep you from your profession. I only said you would not do so in this court, in front of my bench. And if you choose to bring any higher authority into this matter, please allow my clerk at least two weeks to transcribe his very exact notes for such a hearing."

"What good do you think his scribblings will do? The only matter of consequence is what you are trying to do to me. I say again, you have not the authority to deny me access to this court."

"Well, let me remind you of a couple of things, sir. One, I met with you and all the officers of this court within, literally, minutes of my being sworn in. I told you, and all of you then, I would not tolerate dishonesty, abuse of the people we serve, and unpreparedness and its attendant incompetency. Furthermore, Mr. Mayhugh, I am not stopping you from practicing your profession. I'm only denying you access to this court. Go elsewhere, Mayhugh, if you choose. That's none of my affair. But, sir, understand this: you are in the final few moments of your welcome in this court. And, oh yes, Mr. Mayhugh, Mr. Fisher's 'scribblings' have been used, without challenge, in the Supreme Court of these United States. Twice!"

I noticed several heads quickly turned toward J.W. Even his shiny bald head turned red.

"I must remember to apologize to J.W.," I thought. It seemed I had embarrassed him unintentionally.

I turned to J.W. "Mr. Fisher, will you please call the next case?"

The quiet was interrupted only by the sound of Mayhugh slapping the Prather file on J.W.'s table and quickly leaving the courtroom.

As I was leaving the courthouse with Clatilda that evening, I noticed that Jacob wore his shell belt and a holstered gun.

"Expecting trouble, Mr. Webber?" I asked.

"When among the Philistines, partner."

"Been a lot of water under the bridge since first I heard you make that reference."

"For a fact, Will! I was right pleased with the way you handled that Mayhugh gent today. I don't think he has the sand to try anything, but seeing as how you weren't armed, I figured I'd just take out a little insurance."

"What makes you so sure I wasn't armed, Jacob?"

Jacob looked quickly at me, and I simply pulled back the lapel of my coat to reveal the shoulder holster and the pistol it contained.

"Will Jackson!" Clatilda exclaimed, "You mean you actually carried a firearm into your own courtroom?"

"Like a friend of mine once said, 'when among the Philistines.'"

Before hooking her arm in mine, she playfully slapped my shoulder.

"Will, I never knew you to wear a shoulder holster. When did you get it?"

"I had John Terry get it for me. And, Jacob, wait until I show you the Smith and Wesson pistol he got for me! Double action with a four-inch barrel."

"With that short barrel, is it very accurate?"

"Well, Jacob, not for deer or elk, but, in all honesty, I never intended to use it for long-range shooting."

Chapter 7

The balance of my first fortnight as a judge was much less troublesome than the first three days had been. In fact, the last few days I held court in Trinidad, Clatilda and the twins did not attend. They spent their time shopping and getting, better, to know the wives of some of the local politicians. She had a good time and, luckily, my presence was not requested in any social manner.

When we traveled to Alamosa, we were warmly welcomed by Jamie Nava and his daughter, Maria. Maria and Jessie hit it off right away and spent much time doing, what, I never found out.

I had only five cases to hear in Alamosa, and J.W. and I, disposed of them in four days. I continued to be impressed by the little man's competence.

When, we finally started for home, it was as if we were school children, let out for summer vacation.

The last four or five miles to the ranch, we drove in a light snowfall. Jacob rode on ahead to make ready for our arrival. J.W. followed us in his small buggy, seeming not to want us to get too far ahead of him.

When we drove into our dooryard, the house was ablaze with lights, and our family awaited us at the open door. Even the Blalocks were there. Seth Blalock explained later that his wife, Anne had made our Anna Laura promise to send Bud after them at the first sign of our return. Jacob's arrival had provided that sign, and already there was a feast brewing in the kitchen. Jacob, Uncle Buck, Bud, Seth, J.W. and I settled down in the living room while the ladies took over the kitchen and dining area. The twins, with their playing, provided a physical link between the two groups.

J.W. Fisher seemed to be most interested and amused by the twins. It was possible he was only escaping into their company. In all truth, he seemed some put off by the raucous behavior of all of us. Clatilda made every effort she could to see that he was included. But being so busy in the kitchen that evening, her duties as a hostess were somewhat lame, compared to their usual.

Shortly after supper, we all being so tired, the Blalock's went home, and we soon found our beds.

When I stepped out on the porch the next morning, headed for the barn, there sat Uncle Buck and J.W.

"Will, did you know old J. Dub, here, has never ridden horseback?"

"J. Dub?"

"Oh, its all right, sir. Buck, and I have been sitting out here since right after dawn. It's been a little cool, but we've really gotten to know one another."

I couldn't have been more shocked.

"Yeah, Will, it seems we both like to get up with the sun. Like he said, it's been a shade cool, but we didn't want to wake anyone. You suppose Clatilda will be fixing breakfast soon? I'm going to saddle that little piebald gelding, and me and J. Dub are going to see the ranch."

"She was in the kitchen when I came out. I imagine breakfast won't be too long now."

I walked out to the barn, shaking my head in wonder. Of all the people in the world my Uncle Buck would have been the last I'd ever paired up with J.W. Fisher.

I met Jacob as he came from the barn, a full milk bucket in each hand.

"The blamed old Jersey didn't get any better while we were gone! She tried to kick me twice this morning!"

He went on toward the house grumbling about cows in general and the Jersey milk cow in particular.

It was good to be home!

I heard Clatilda's call and returned to the house for breakfast.

As we were finishing the meal, Clatilda said she had forgotten to tell me something the night before.

"Will, Anna Laura said Bishop Terry told her last Sunday to have you come in and see him when you got back. She said he didn't tell her what it was about, just that it wasn't urgent, but, to come as soon as it was convenient."

"Well, I need to go over the court's docket for Durango and Pagosa Springs as soon as I can, to get it out of the way. But it would seem Uncle Buck has taken over J.W.'s time, at least for today. I see they are already leaving the barn. So I guess I'll go in today."

"All right, if you'll wait a little bit, I'll take Anna Laura to school. I have some things I need to get from the store and maybe I'll visit around town today, and bring her back with me when school is out."

I got to the store in town to find John Terry busy with two drummers from Kansas City. So, I went into the bank to see Abraham Terry, the manager. John and I own the bank and hired his nephew to manage it for us. It took only a few minutes to see the bank was doing well, indeed. In fact, it shamed me a little to see just how much money we were making off our friends and neighbors.

"Abraham, do you suppose we should lower our interest rate a tad? We seem to be making an awful lot of money."

"Now, Mr. Jackson, you and Uncle John bullied me into lowering the rates once. We now have people from as far away as Alamosa and Gunnison inquiring about loans. Our rates are low enough. But I have wanted to talk to you about something. As you can see, we are accumulating quite a surplus. We need to put it to work. I could generate quite a profit if we properly invested it."

"Boy, is that all you think about, making more money?"

He sat and looked at me for a moment.

"Mr. Jackson, oh, I'm sorry, it's Judge Jackson now, isn't it? Sir, what is it you think I do for a living?"

"Why, you run this bank. And a darn good job you seem to be doing, too."

"Sir, my real reason for taking the rather generous salary you and Uncle John pay me is to make money. You could hire a clerk to count the money we receive, and Uncle John knows our customers well enough to approve most loans. But, the investment of the bank's surplus capital is where I earn my money."

"Whoa, now, what investments are you talking about?"

"For instance, three months ago, the widow Lester decided to join her sister in Provo, and I arranged for the bank to buy her place. I then sold it two weeks ago to Jack Swenson. The bank almost doubled its investment. I have, over the past few years, made several such transactions. In fact, that red wheeled surrey, your wife is so fond of, made the bank almost a hundred dollars profit!"

"I thought we bought that from the store!"

"No sir, you bought it through the store but from the bank."

"You know, Abraham, I'm not sure you're not moving a little fast for my liking."

"Judge Jackson, I maintain very careful records of everything I do. I do nothing in haste, and never anything that jeopardizes a dime of the bank's money. I don't think you realize, sir, the importance of the bank to this area. And, that brings me to the real reason I've been wanting to see you. I've already talked to Uncle John about this. The bank in Monte Vista is for sale. Their assets are only about half of ours, but I believe careful management can improve that, and rather quickly."

"Wait a minute, son. If we bought that bank, providing we could afford to, who would run it?"

"Sir, my brother is currently working as a loan officer in a bank in Salt Lake City. I have written to him, and he and his wife would be happy to come to Monte Vista. The salary he says he would require is only a little more than half what the owner of the bank in Monte Vista is drawing now."

"You've looked into this pretty carefully haven't you?"

"Yes, sir. I tend not to go off half-cocked. What I would present to you and Uncle John is a complete proposal. Even to the three to five hundred dollars the bank would save by having you handle the legal aspects of the sale and transfer of ownership."

I stood and looked at this young man with new respect. And, I must admit, with some misgiving. I wasn't that certain I was completely comfortable with his ambition. John and I might have to figure a way to get a little firmer grip on the banking side of our lives. Up to now it had never been more to me than a way to help our friends after that terrible blizzard a few years previous. It now seemed to have taken a life of its own and its growth amazed me.

I told Abraham I'd get back to him after I'd had a chance to talk to John. He seemed quite comfortable with this and escorted me out of his office. I suddenly realized I hadn't known he had a separate office. My conscious memory of the bank was one large room dominated by a huge safe, adjoined the store. I looked around. I couldn't see the safe.

"Abraham, where's the safe?"

"It's behind that south wall, sir. When we remodeled last year, we built a special brick room for it."

"I'm going to have to come here more often," I thought. "It might be interesting to see what's happening to my money."

I went into the store, which no longer had a door directly into the bank. I was required to step out onto the porch from the bank, then into the front door of the store.

John was now free and quickly came to greet me.

"Well, Judge Jackson, welcome home. I'm happy to see you. There are a couple of things I've been waiting to talk to you about!"

"One of them had better concern the bank!" I replied.

"As a matter of fact, it does. I see you've already talked to Abraham."

"Yeah, and I'll tell you, Bishop, I'm just a bit uneasy."

Smiling, he took my arm. "Let's go up where we won't be disturbed and talk about it."

John had an office perch located at the rear of his store. Stairs led a dozen steps above the main level of the store. Not large but sufficient for him to have a degree of privacy from the activities of the main floor of the mercantile.

When we were settled, John asked about my new job.

"Frankly, John, I'm still not sure it's what I really want. I know it's what I've worked and studied for, but I just don't know if I'm ready."

"If not now, when, Will?"

"Been talking to Clatilda?"

"Not recently, but I watched you work so hard for this, and I think you will make a good judge."

"Well, I've committed myself to at least give it a fair trial. I hate to start something, then quit in the middle."

"Will, we need to talk about the bank and Abraham's plans, but that's not the real reason I wanted to see you. We've got a problem developing, and I'd not like to see it get out of hand. There has been a fellow coming in here recently who says he bought several thousand acres south of here, and he claims he will be moving his cattle here from over east of Walsenburg. He claims to have a herd of over three thousand head. He says he wants to use our village and this store as his source of supply. Furthermore, Ray Bumgartner, from just across the pass west of here, has been in and placed two very large orders in the last month. He says it's just too far to go on in to Gunnison. I don't know if you know him, but he has a good sized outfit. Says he runs almost four thousand head."

"Sounds like nothing but good news so far, John. Is there some sort of problem?"

"Yes, and I'm surprised you didn't notice it when you came home. There's two new businesses the other side of the river."

"What kind of businesses?"

"A saloon and a blacksmith shop."

"That's what I wanted to talk to you about, Will. Also, there's talk about the saloon keeper building some sort of hotel over there."

"Well, that sounds like a little solid growth. That's not going to be a problem, is it?"

"Will, you've been around, some. Did you ever see a saloon keeper, that owned an adjacent hotel, who could resist bringing in a few 'girls'?"

"Whoa! You're talking about a saloon and a blacksmith shop, and that's going to grow overnight into a hotel and a bawdy house?"

"Will, I kept a store back east in two different towns. That's exactly how it happens."

"John, I hate to see some such happen, but, from where I sit, I don't know what can be done about it."

"That's what I wanted to talk to you about. The first thing I believe, should happen, is the appointment of a peace officer for this area."

"For our little village?"

"It's not 'our little village' anymore, Will. As I've been telling you, we are in the way of becoming a trading center for fifty or seventy-five miles in any direction. That means more people, most of whom will not think as we do. What's more, if we allow that area south of the river to build up helter-skelter, we may soon be an uncomfortable minority in an area we settled specifically to get away from that sort of thing. Which could now happen in our own backyard."

"Well, I suppose we could find someone to act as sort of a Marshal, and it is in my power, as a judge, to create the job."

"How about Jacob Webber?"

"As a lawman?"

"Yes, why not?"

"Knowing Jacob, as I do, I just wouldn't have thought of him."

"He's been with you and Clatilda for some time now. He's honest enough, isn't he?"

"I suspect I'd take his word for anything."

"He always seems to go armed, like you used to. Is he any good with a firearm?"

"Well, I'll just say this. What he can't cover with quality, he can bury with quantity!"

John looked at me without understanding.

"Don't worry, John, if Jacob took the job, he would handle it. But that won't keep undesirables away. Maybe keep them from getting out of hand, but not away."

"That's fine. Now I understand you have talked to Abraham about his plan to buy the Monte Vista Bank?"

"Yeah, he brought it up, but I shied away from it. I told him I wanted to talk to you first."

"I'm not completely for it. I have another investment in mind."

"Oh?"

"Yes, Will, lets use the bank's surplus to build that hotel. Only, let's build it just a little closer to the river. That way, we can better control its activities."

"Do you think a regular hotel would make money here?"

"Will, I've been watching the past few months. We average three to four parties camping along the river every week. Some are families with wagons, but most are horseback. Some are cowboys, who probably would camp out if there were a half dozen hotels nearby. But a large number are travelers who come here in the morning for food. I've sent most over to widow James. She's been glad to fix breakfast, and is much happier for the money. Will, we could let her run a small café in the hotel and solve two problems right there."

"John, you're going too fast. First Abraham hits me with the banks profits. Now you come on with a full-blown plan to spend those profits and probably much more."

"Will, did Abraham show you just how much money the bank has above and beyond any needs it might have?"

"No, he showed me a couple of pieces of paper, but frankly, I didn't really look closely at them."

"You should have. You would have seen that we could build the hotel, a new bridge over the river closer to us, here and still have nearly enough to go ahead and buy the Monte Vista Bank!"

"And we've made that much money off our friends and neighbors?"

"No, Will. I'm sure Abraham told you of some of the investments he's made."

"Only the purchase and resale of the Lester place. Oh, yes, and my red-wheeled surrey."

"Will, the young man has a real knack for making money. I believe if he keeps up for the next five years as he has for the past few, you and I will be moderately wealthy men."

"John, that's not why we started the bank."

"Will, we now offer the lowest interest rates that can be found between Pueblo and Salt Lake City. There's not a soul in this valley who's been turned down for any reasonable monetary request they have made on the bank. We've been fair and taken care of our people. What's more, I have insisted upon the same principle in dealing with those outside our valley with whom the bank has had dealings."

"Well, this is something I am going to have to think about, John."

"Don't think too long, Will. We need to at least have our hotel started before that saloon keeper gets settled well enough to start his hotel."

"What's to keep him from bringing his 'girls' into his saloon?"

"Not one thing. But, at least decent travelers won't have to share their accommodation with that kind of trash."

"I'll think on it, John, and I'll let you know by Sunday. All right?"

"That'll be fine, Will. And, also, will you talk to Mr. Webber about the other matter?"

"Yeah, I will, John, and I'll tell you something else: I'll be tempted to sell tickets to that conversation! Me, asking Jacob Webber to wear a badge!"

Chapter 8

The two days after my conversation with John Terry were spent trying to catch J.W. Fisher between the "horseback riding lessons" Uncle Buck was giving him. I wanted to set the court dockets for Durango and Pagosa Springs so we might finish and return from that area before any major winter storms set in.

It took the whole two days to get the dockets set and ready. J.W. and Uncle Buck had become fast friends and announced their intent to visit the Medinas, over by Saguache, to see if they could buy one of their fine horses for J.W.. Uncle Buck had told J.W. he could keep the horse in with his, Uncle Buck's, stock right here on the ranch. No further consideration was given to whose ranch this livestock was being run on. More and more, I felt myself losing control of more and more.

It was not until after the dockets were set that I asked Clatilda to take a walk with me. As was our custom, we strolled up to the little family cemetery.

Little was said on the way up, and for a short time after we arrived.

We had been standing by our little Sarah's grave for but a few minutes, when Clatilda turned to me.

"What is it, Will?"

I turned and looked down at this woman who knew me only too well.

"How would you like being married to a hotel keeper?"

"You asked me a similar question once about a banker. That turned out all right."

As we stood there in the warm autumn sun, I explained everything Abraham, Bishop Terry and I had talked about. The only emotion Clatilda showed, during the entire explanation, was a suppressed titter when I got to the part about Jacob being a lawman. I asked her if she thought he would not do well as such.

"Oh, I think he'd be a fine lawman. The only thing is, I'd like to be present when you bring it up to him."

"That's about what I told John."

We talked the morning away and wound up much as I had expected.

"Will, if you and John think this will be good for us and the community, go ahead. When would you start building your new town?"

"I don't know. I told John, I'd give him my answer Sunday. I suspect we'll decide the first of next week."

"You'll have to hurry, won't you? We'll have to start for Durango by Thursday at the latest."

"We'll see. The main thing, on my mind now is to talk to Jacob."

"When do you intend to do that?"

"I'll talk to him right after we eat. Maybe he will be in a good mood then."

"If you'd told me sooner, I'd have fixed that stew he likes so well!"

"Let's not gang up on poor old Jacob too much. He's in for a tough enough afternoon, as it is."

After dinner, I asked Jacob to stay for a minute, as I had something I needed to see him about.

This was not unusual as, often, this was the way I had of giving Jacob instructions about the work on the ranch.

I had him come back to my office with me.

"You know, Will," he began, after we were seated, "you've had this office, now, what, about eight or ten years?"

"Just about that."

"I still feel like I should take off my boots when I come in here."

"I've got to be honest with you, Jacob, there are times I feel uncomfortable here."

"Even after all the time you've spent in here?"

"Even so. I just can't get past the fact that I'll always be a cowboy. And, this is just not where a cowboy ought to spend his days."

"Yeah, but Will, you're a judge now!"

"Sure, but my place is in a saddle, not in front of a bunch of people who wouldn't know which end of a branding iron to grab."

"Yeah, I've been watching J. Dub with his riding lessons. But I'll tell you something, that little guy is tough. I saw him get throwed twice from that new pony he bought from Pete Medina. He just climbed right back up. He's getting that horse pretty well under control."

"Jacob, getting things 'under control' is just what I wanted to talk to you about."

"What's wrong, Will? I thought the ranch was running real good. That Ballard kid's turned into a real hand, and Uncle Buck looks like he's going to live forever. I'll swear that old man just gets tougher as he ages."

"No, Jacob, it's not the ranch I'm talking about."

"What, then?"

"Jacob, do you know about the new saloon that's been built south of town?"

"Yeah, and I don't like it!"

I looked at the man for a moment.

"Jacob, I would have thought that would not bother you."

"Those people got no right bringing that kind of place among our folks!"

"Our folks?"

"Aw, Will, you know what I mean!"

"Yes, indeed, I do. And that's what I want to talk to you about. Jacob, I'm afraid the time has come for our area to have a peace officer. I'd like to talk to you about wearing that badge."

"You want me to be a lawman?"

"That's what I'd hoped."

"All right."

"All right?"

"You said you want me to be a lawman. If that's what you want then that's what I'll do."

"Jacob, if you and Clatilda, and I live to be a hundred years old, I'll not understand either of you!"

"What's wrong with Miss Clatilda?"

"Not one thing! In fact, of all the people in this world, you and she are the best."

"You will tell me what you expect of me when I start wearing this badge?"

"Absolutely, Jacob. In fact don't plan anything for yourself next Monday. You, J.W. and I will go to town and sit down with John Terry and work the whole matter out."

Jacob left by the back door to my office while I went back to the kitchen to tell Clatilda, as I had promised, how Jacob had reacted to my request.

"He said 'all right,' he would be a lawman."

"No argument, no nothing?"

"Not a thing. Just asked if that's what I wanted. When I said it was, he said 'all right.' He, J.W. and I are going in to get it settled Monday."

"Why, J.W., Will?"

"I will dictate Jacob's commission to him and he can record it, and also he can advise me as to the proper form. I'm sure he has been through this or something like it in his long service as a recorder."

"I cannot believe Jacob just said 'all right.' I kept expecting to hear shouting, or at least laughter from back there!'

"Frankly, I didn't know what to expect. I'll say one thing, though, I fully expected it to take an hour or more to convince him. Our Mr. Webber never ceases to amaze me!"

"When will you set everything up?"

"Like I said, we'll all go see John, Monday. We should be able to set everything up that one day. Frankly I think it should be a subject of discussion in priesthood meeting Sunday."

"Do you think there might be any problem with the brethren?"

"I don't think so. I suspect John has already spoken to some, if not several, about this."

"What will Jacob be, Will? A Marshal, Sheriff, or what?"

"That remains to be seen. He won't be much good as a marshal unless we incorporate the area south of town into the village and even that may not do any good. We may have to set up as an incorporated township, then appoint Jacob as marshal of the township. We'll just have to see how it falls out."

Chapter 9

Sunday morning, I was anxious to see John Terry. I met him just outside the church. When I told him I was ready to go on all issues, including even, the purchase of the Monte Vista Bank, he was pleased. He offered to call a special priesthood meeting that afternoon so all might know of our plans.

That meeting brought a few surprises. It was unanimously agreed that the four actions should happen immediately. The bridge was the first order of business for most. Construction on the hotel was to start as soon as Jed Adair's sawmill could turn out the lumber after cutting the timbers for the hotel bridge.

It was agreed to hold an election as soon as possible, to allow for incorporation of the village. A vote was taken and a name assigned to our little town. It was to be known as Goshen.

And, finally, after the incorporation election was complete, the job of town marshal was to be offered to Jacob Webber.

All of this was handled with so little fanfare. I was sure I should do some research to make sure everything was legal.

It just seemed to me that anything involving so much could not be legal, if done so simply.

After some discussion, it was decided the election for incorporation would be held after my return from Durango and Pagosa Springs.

On the way home that evening I explained what was to take place, to Clatilda.

"Will, who will own the hotel and bridge?" she asked.

"Why, I suppose the bridge will become public property, and I suppose the bank will own the hotel."

"What about the people who build the bridge and the hotel? Will the bank pay them day wages?"

"You know, we never even discussed that. Everyone was so excited over the whole project that wages, or even cost, never came up."

"Will, would you mind if I made a suggestion?"

"Would it matter?"

She playfully punched my shoulder, "Don't get smart, cowboy! Just remember I've got money in that bank, also."

"What's your suggestion?"

"Why don't you have the bank hold fifty-one percent of the hotel by putting up the money for the land and materials, and those who build the bridge and hotel earn a part of the remaining forty-nine percent according to the amount of labor they contribute?"

"You know, that's about the smartest idea to come out of this whole shebang. I'll talk to John and Abraham tomorrow. I'm sure they will go along with it, because, you know what that will do?"

"Sure! That will free up enough money to allow for the purchase of the Monte Vista Bank, and maybe even have some left over."

"Ma'am, would you please tell me when that brain of yours ever shuts down?"

"Cowboy, as far as your welfare is concerned, it never does."

"Then you think we'd be wise to go ahead with the Monte Vista Bank?"

"With Abraham and his brother watching over it, I don't see how you could go wrong."

Thus it was that a panhandle cowboy, whose greatest ambition had once been two meals a day, a bed in some buggy bunkhouse and thirty dollars a month, became a man of property. Part-owner of two banks, a hotel, ranch, and, through his wife, partner in a thriving mercantile store. I leave out the part about my law practice and my position as judge. It was my honest opinion that I would probably be found out some day and lose that whole set up. Oh, well, as Uncle Buck had said, once, "with a spud farmer on one side of me and a rich wife on the other," I probably won't ever go hungry.

Chapter 10

Jacob, J.W., and I arrived at the store that Monday, just as John was opening for business. We left Jacob and J.W. in the store, while John and I went to the bank, where we discussed Clatilda's plan. It took no longer than my explanation for both John and Abraham to agree to the plan. John had a very good idea. He suggested we have Jacob serve as timekeeper on the two projects. That way we could have an accurate record of donated labor, and Jacob would be given a good chance to better know the men of our community. This while also serving as town marshal.

Abraham said, with our permission, he would get in touch with his brother and have him and his wife come as soon as possible. That way his brother, whose name I found to be William, would be on hand throughout the Monte Vista Bank purchase negotiations. This, he said, would make William better acquainted with the overall proposition. Abraham said he would have to put his brother on the payroll immediately and asked if John or I had any objections.

"Is there money for this?" I asked.

"Yes, sir," Abraham answered. "I included such in the planning for the purchase."

"Do it!" I said. "Also, are there any other things we need to know about the Monte Vista Bank?"

"Well, there is one thing. The building is made of adobe and could really use a good coat of white wash."

"Is there, somewhere, money for that too?" again, I asked.

"Oh, yes, sir, I'm sure I could find the money for that."

"You know, Abraham," I said, "if it became necessary to build a new outhouse for that bank, I suspect you could 'find' the money for it."

As solemn as a judge, he leaned forward. "Do you think we should have a new outhouse built?"

John and I were laughing about that all the way back to the store.

By the time we presented the plan to Jacob and J.W., it was all over, but for the shouting.

Jacob agreed, J.W. said he could have the necessary election notices ready for posting before we left for Durango, and between the two of us we could have the incorporation agreement ready to submit to the territorial government by the time we returned from Durango. We left John's store before eleven that morning.

John was to start Jed Adair cutting bridge timbers immediately, and with any luck at all, have the bridge completed before the river iced over. As for the hotel that might go a little slower. It depended entirely upon the weather.

The rest of the week was busy what with my getting ready to be gone for at least three weeks.

J.W. and Uncle Buck informed me that J.W. would be going horseback on this trip. In questioning J.W., I found he actually had no home. He lived in one hotel or another and carried everything he owned in his buggy. He bought his paper and other supplies he needed in his job in whatever town he found himself.

Clatilda reacted almost predictably when we discussed this. The next morning she asked J.W. how he liked the room in which he had slept the past two days. He responded, somewhat hesitantly, that it was just fine.

"Good, Mr. Fisher, when you and Will return from Durango, I will have more satisfactory furnishings in there. In the meantime, you can leave what you won't need on this trip in that room."

"Oh, but Mrs. Jackson, I couldn't do that!"

"Why not, Mr. Fisher?"

"I couldn't just move in."

"And, why not?"

J.W. sputtered and stammered for a couple of minutes until Jacob spoke up.

"Consider yourself lucky, J. Dub, she makes me stay in the barn!"

"Jacob Webber, I've asked you repeatedly if you wouldn't be more comfortable in the house!"

"I know, ma'am, but you know I'm right comfortable in my room. And, besides, Will would holler on me if I brought all my hardware in your house."

"Hardware?" J.W. asked, seemingly glad to have the attention turned to someone else.

"Yes, J.W.," I said, "I'm sure you don't know it, but Jacob only weighs sixty pounds when he takes out all the guns and knives he carries on his person."

"Mr. Webber, just how many guns do you carry?" Anna Laura spoke up.

"Now, Miss Anna Laura, don't you worry, I'd never let anyone harm you, even if I have to carry twice as many as I do now," Jacob said.

"Jacob, that sorry-looking horse you ride couldn't carry twice as much iron as he totes now, when you climb on him," Uncle Buck spoke up.

We continued to tease Jacob for some while longer. However, as we were finishing breakfast, Clatilda sent Bud to the barn to find a clean crate for J.W. to store his possessions in, at least, as she said, "until suitable furniture arrives."

J.W. looked at me, with some bewilderment.

"Friend, there's not a thing I can, or will, do. You have been adopted by Clatilda. And, believe me, J.W., there are many worse things in this world."

"But, Mrs. Jackson, you must at least let me pay you rent for the room."

"Very well, sir," Clatilda said, much to the amazement of everyone at the breakfast table, the monthly rent for that room and the occasional meal you might take at my table will be one thousand dollars, sir. If you cannot afford that sum, sir, please accept my invitation to be our most welcome guest."

J.W. looked around the table, as all seated there just smiled at his consternation.

"I have surely landed amongst strange people," he finally said.

"Yeah, and ain't it great!" Jacob said, getting up from his chair. "If all the palaver is over, come on Bud, you and I have a bunch of cattle to get moved today. We can't sit around like a bunch of judges and what not!"

J.W. and I left for Durango Thursday morning. Both of us horseback and leading one pack horse. I had convinced Clatilda not to come. The weather was soon to surely worsen and travel through the country where we were headed could be chancy, at best.

As it turned out, we couldn't have asked for better weather all the way to Durango.

I asked J.W., along the way, why he had scheduled court in Durango before Pagosa Springs, in that we went right through Pagosa on the way to Durango.

"Judge Claus had a niece in Pagosa that he would visit, so he liked to have more time to spend with her after finishing in Durango."

"Well this time we'll schedule Pagosa first on the next trip. Will that be all right with you?"

"However you would like it, judge."

"Will!"

"Very well, Will."

Chapter 11

Durango was quick and easy. I found that only two of the attorneys who followed my court were there. There was one case involving petty theft and another in which a drunken miner had caused a considerable amount of damage to a local saloon and a mercantile. The two businesses were owned by the same person and separated only by a sheet wall ending in a large archway. It was through this archway that the miner had thrown several chairs, three of the saloon's customers and a faro dealer. The latter receiving much more damage than any of the other objects sailing through that opening.

One of the attorneys acted as the miner's defense. When he was examining the miner, he asked him why he had thrown all those people and things through the archway.

"They were in my way," was the man's terse response.

"Where you going that you couldn't go round these people and chairs?"

"I was trying to get to the faro dealer."

"Why?" asked the prosecutor.

"Because he was running a crooked table."

"Why didn't you just complain to the saloon keeper?"

"It was his table."

"Did you complain to him?"

"I did. And he told me to go somewhere and sleep it off. I didn't throw him through that door."

"What did you do?"

"I left him behind the stove."

"Did you hurt him?"

"Don't know. Sure aimed to!"

"Was it then you attacked the faro dealer?"

"Didn't 'attack' him, I just throwed him out of the saloon."

"What about the chairs and other people?"

"They was at a table the faro dealer was hiding behind."

"Just how did you know the faro dealer was dishonest?"

"Don't know if he was dishonest."

"I thought you said he was."

"I said he was crooked."

"That's the same thing."

"If that's a fact, then he was crooked and dishonest, to boot."

"Do you know where the faro dealer is now?"

"Yeah, I hear when he got well, he left town."

"What about the bartender?"

"Don't know. I ain't been back to his saloon."

"Do you realize you hurt several people and caused over two hundred dollars damage?"

"I reckon."

"What do you intend doing about it?"

"Well, I thought to go up to Leadville and get me a job in the silver mines. Then maybe I could send a few dollars every payday, until things got set right."

The attorney then turned his client over to the other attorney, a C. W. Hastings, whom I had appointed to prosecute the case.

"Your honor, my investigation of this matter has essentially confirmed what the defendant has said, and no one has come forth to complain of any personal injury. As Mr. Hoskins has actually admitted to his part and offered to make restitution, I would move for a directed verdict involving only the restitution of two hundred eight dollars and thirty-seven cents to be paid, by installments, to the Golden Eagle Mercantile Company."

I looked at the miner.

"Mr. Hoskins, will you pay for the damages you caused?"

"That's what I said, wasn't it?"

"Mr. Hoskins, I'd be more inclined to go along with you if you were a little more sorry for what you have done."

"Judge, on the money I make in the mines, I can't get much sorrier than two hundred, eight dollars and thirty-seven cents. If you'll let me get up to Leadville so I can get me a job, I'll pay for the damages. I promise."

"That's good enough for me, Mr. Hoskins. Mr. Fisher, please provide Mr. Hoskins with the saloon owner's name and address so he may know where to send the money."

We spent only a week in Durango, during which time there were two light snows. The ride back to Pagosa Springs was cold and windy but, otherwise, not unpleasant.

We had only two cases in Pagosa Springs. Both were minor, and we spent only one day there. The morning we left, the weather was dark and heavily overcast. It started to spit snow before we were out of sight of the town. J.W. asked if I thought maybe we should go back to town and wait out the storm. Foolishly, I said we should go on. I told him we'd been lucky winding up the circuit so quickly, and I welcomed an early return home.

It continued to snow, not too hard, but steady. It took all day and far into the evening to reach the summit of Wolf Creek Pass. There was an inn, of sorts, on the north side of the summit. It was after midnight by the time we'd cared for our horses. There was little to eat, so we settled for cold beans and stale cornbread. We were both ready for the bed.

I awoke, feeling it should be morning except the room was pitch black. I felt for and found a cup of matches on the bedside table. When I looked at my watch, I was astounded to see it to be after eight. I got up, lit the lamp and dressed. J.W. was downstairs when I came down.

"I'm afraid we have a problem, Judge. There was quite a storm last night."

He lead me to the door. Opening it, we were faced with a howling blizzard and quite an accumulation of snow.

I took a few steps out into the yard. The snow was up to my knees and coming down at an angle, beaten by the wind. As I turned back to the door, I was momentarily disoriented. I made I am sure a complete circle before I felt J.W.'s hand on my arm.

"This way, Judge."

I felt almighty foolish as I followed J.W. back into the inn.

"It almost happened to me earlier, sir. I stepped out and with the wind swirling around, I made two false starts before I got back in."

"That's the first time that ever happened to me, J.W. It proves one thing; We'll not be starting out until this lets up."

We turned back into the room to discover four other men standing at a makeshift bar.

"Be a while before anyone leaves won't it, mister?" spoke up the bartender.

"Do you have enough supplies to keep us for the length of this storm?" I asked.

"Mister, I run this place for eight years, now. I got enough dry stuff to last til this time next year, and what's more, I got four steers out back eating on a pile of hay that fourteen steers couldn't get rid of in a year. So, yeah, mister, ain't none of us going hungry. Also, I got enough liquor to keep us all half drunk, all winter. And that's not even counting two barrels of that 'who hit John' corn whiskey I run off myself. Let you have a shot of that for a nickel."

I looked at J.W., and smiled, "I don't think we'll be needing any of that liquor, but it is good news, indeed, that we won't starve."

We didn't starve. Roast beef, beans and cornbread got a little old in the next ten days. Especially, as that was the only food available, three times every day.

I found it hard to believe the depth of the snow. In most flat areas it was waist deep, and there were precious few flat areas.

It finally stopped snowing and cleared off. J.W. and I ventured out to see if we couldn't get going. While we were tromping around, an older man came out of the inn and joined us.

"Thinking of leaving?" he asked.

"Well, yes and no. We'd like to leave, but I'm in no such hurry to kill a horse in this."

"Mister, you going north or south?" he asked.

"North, towards Del Norte," I responded.

"Then, you'd best go east, and get into the black timber. Ain't no way you can get straight down off this mountain," he said pointing east, "You'd get right into heavy timber. Have to wind around some, but, if you're careful and watch for drop-offs, the snow ain't going to be much more than knee-deep. You got a compass, Mister?"

"No, I haven't," I said.

"I have, Will. A good one," J.W. said.

"Good, cause you'll need one. First go east through that timber. After about three hours, if you're making good headway, turn north. Drop you right into the valley, not five miles west of Del Norte. But, be careful. With the drifts and all, you could step off a cliff right easy and never know what hit you."

"You been that way, friend?" I asked.

"Four times so far. This ain't the first time I got caught on this mountain."

"You going that way anytime soon?" I asked.

"Nope, I'm headed south. I'm gonna get myself out of this country. Going down to Santa Fe. I got kin down there. I figure to snuggle up to their fire and never wade another snow drift for the rest of my days."

J.W. and I spent the rest of that day getting ourselves ready for what we figured would be a rough trip.

Bright and early the next morning, J.W. and I set out, east from the inn. We got into heavy timber in less than a mile. Our friend was right about the snow. He was also right about drop-offs. We, twice within the first hour, had to double back from cliffs too steep to get down. What we hadn't been told was the amount of down timber. At least twice, every hour or so, J.W. and I had to find our way around downed timber so thick as to be impenetrable.

I began to notice how nervous J.W. was becoming as the day wore on. Finally, in the late afternoon, we stopped to let our horses blow and rest awhile.

"J.W., have you ever camped out in this kind of weather?"

"No, and the prospect doesn't please me."

"Well, it's not a lot of fun, but it can be done, and with at least some comfort. The trick is to find the right place."

"What would be 'the right place'?"

"Anywhere that offers shelter. A cave, back under blown-down timber is often all right. Just about anywhere you can be sheltered and be able to have a fire."

"Will, would that place down there work?" J.W. said pointing about a quarter of a mile down the slope from where we stood.

It was easy to see the cave would do more than just "work." It appeared perfect.

As early as it was, we headed right for that cave.

We found a half dozen dead snags laying around the opening and in less than an hour, we were nearly as well set up as we had been in the inn.

It was cold that night. So cold, we kept a good fire going all night. But, aside from tending the fire, we both got a good warm night's rest.

We had traveled east until a little after noon, then turned north. I felt we should reach Del Norte about dark the second day.

I got up about dawn, as it was my turn to feed the fire. I looked out at the mouth of the cave. It was as if a white curtain had been drawn. The snow was falling straight down and heavily.

I stepped to the opening. There was only a few inches of new snow in our tracks of the previous evening.

It took J.W. and I less than ten minutes to be on our way.

The snow was still heavy and coming down steadily, but there was no wind.

Within an hour of leaving the cave, I knew we were in trouble. The snow was coming down faster and heavier, and the wind was picking up. I started to look for shelter, and meanwhile keeping an eye on J.W., who seemed to be having more and more trouble with his mount.

There were lots of downed trees, but few down in such a way as to offer shelter. I could see no caves or rock outcroppings at all. And, as far as I could see, no place to hide from the relentless snowfall and deepening drifts.

I was also becoming concerned about J.W. and his horse. He was not, yet, a good enough rider to be exposed to the terrain and weather we were experiencing. He was unable, yet, to come to that balance of trust between horse and rider that allows the animal to do that, of which, it is more capable than the man.

We continued on down the mountain, always in a northerly direction. The drifts were increasing, and I grew more concerned that one would cover a precipice over which J.W., or we both, might fall.

Finally, I became so concerned, I began to look around for any seemly place we might stop. I suddenly realized I had been leading us around an aspen grove. I stopped and looked closer into the thick stand of white leafless trees. They were growing so close together it was almost impossible to get a horse between them. I knew the ground would be littered with fallen, stripped poles. I made my decision and, while doing so, cursed my stupidity for not seeing the solution to our problem sooner.

I waited for J.W. to ride up beside me, then, over the howl of the wind, explained my plan.

We forced our horses into the grove, finally having to dismount and lead them.

Once, into the thicker growth, I kicked around and started pulling the dead aspen trunks from under the snow. J.W. helped, and soon we had begun a large, tee-pee like, structure. Almost as quickly as we stood the poles up, the snow began to seal the cracks between them. When we had the best structure we could make, I had J.W. help me pull some of the living trees over to make a sort of tent for the animals. It was crude and leaked snow like a sieve, but it kept the worst of the weather from the three horses.

We took the tarp from our pack horse and stretched it over the northwest side of our teepee, thus stopping most of the wind. After we got a small fire going on an area in the center of our shelter, we began to thaw out.

"Will, how long do you think we might have to stay here?" J.W. asked after we'd settled down.

"Only until the storm lets up. I would suspect, this time of year, we will not see too many clear days on this mountain. What we'll have to do is get ourselves down into the valley just as soon as the snow stops. And, my friend, that could be an hour from now or a week."

I was grateful for the beans and cornbread provided by the innkeeper.

J.W. sat, very quietly, for better than an hour. Neither of us did anything beyond boiling a little jerky over our fire to make a sort of strong, watery soup which we both enjoyed.

"Will," J.W. finally said, "you know, if anything happens that we don't get down off this mountain and out of this storm, I'd much rather go out this way, than in some strange barren hotel room."

I looked over at this little man that, lately, had become so much a part of my life. Such a comfortable, quiet, easy part of my life.

"J.W., I think we'll make it. It's going to be rough, but I don't believe either one of us is going to die on this trip."

"Oh, I hope not. But, Will, I've felt more alive in the past day and a half than I ever have in my entire life. I think I am finally beginning to understand the love so many have for this country. For the past ten years, I now realize, I've been only a spectator to my existence. Not unlike those people we see in the courtroom, day after day. Not participating in any way but just watching others live."

"You know, J.W., that's one of the things that bothers me most about my job. I love the law and have thought for awhile that my greatest ambition was to get where I am now. But, frankly, when I sit in the courtroom, I feel like I have missed all the action, and, if you will, the fun. Everything really worth seeing has already happened. We're like a swamper in a saloon. All the fun's over, and we're just cleaning up the mess. But here, this is where life has real meaning. This is where the fun really is."

"Yes, Will, and the strange part, that I only now begin to understand, is that even though you're here with me, this is really a very personal experience."

"Mr. Fisher, no matter what happens, it has been a real pleasure to know you."

"Likewise, Will Jackson."

J.W. and I spend the rest of that day and far into the night in our aspen tent. I awakened and got up to feed the fire, when I noticed the wind had died down. I peeked out to see clear skies and more stars than I knew existed.

I quickly awakened J.W. and we packed up, saddled our horses and headed down off that mountain.

The rest of our trip was somewhat of an anticlimax. We rode into Del Norte late that afternoon cold and hungry, but little worse for the wear.

We spent that night in the hotel at Del Norte and the next morning started for the ranch.

The storm J.W. and I went through had to have been widespread, for we rode through snow all the way home. We were not due in Alamosa for five weeks, so we looked forward to a good long period at the ranch.

Chapter 12

JW and I went to town the first morning we were home. We knew things had gone well in our absence for we had ridden across the new bridge the night before. It had appeared to be a fine stout structure capable of handling even the heaviest wagons.

John Terry told us the foundation stones for the hotel had been laid just before the snow hit four days before. He said the first load of lumber for the hotel was due to be delivered that day. He further told us there was some excitement about the impending election. I couldn't believe how fast the bridge had gone up and told him so. He said there had been few in the community that had not worked on it.

It was good to be home. Work on the ranch went well, and we helped some of the men in town to build Jacob a small office and a jail room, of sorts, adjacent to the bank. We joined the building to the south wall of the bank. Our little village was beginning to take on the appearance of a town.

It was decided to extend the town limits beyond the saloon, in order to include all businesses. The saloon owner complained to John Terry, but he had no support.

We found that among his many other talents, J.W. was capable of surveying and setting the town boundaries. John had a useable transit in the store. So we had metes and bounds to submit with our articles for incorporation.

By Easter, the walls and roof of the Goshen Hotel were up, and work continued on the inside of the building. It was not a really imposing structure. There was to be a lobby, small café, and ten rooms. The craftsmanship of some of the men began to show as there developed sort of competition to see who could do their work better than others.

The Sunday after Easter we all met Effie Johansson. She was Hester Turner's niece and a widow. Hester introduced her as the daughter of her older brother. Effie's husband had been killed by a run-away team, and as she had no other relatives, save Pearl Stanton, and Jess and Hester were closer to her previous home. She was not some poor relative dependent on the Turners, for she came to church in her own surrey, drawn by the finest pair of matched gray horses I've ever seen. She seemed a little standoffish, and I assumed it to be due to her husband's recent death. But, Jess Turner told me, after services, that her husband had been dead almost a year. She had been long in disposing of their farm and deciding where to live. Jess said there had been quite a struggle between the two sisters Pearl Stanton and Hester Turner, to see with whom Effie would live. Jess said he didn't know whether he was that happy Hester had won out. When I asked why, he just stared off into the distance.

"Effie is so much like Pearl and Hester she could be their daughter. Two, like Hester in the same house will be, at the very best, interesting. And, to top it all off, she is said, by Hester, to have 'second sight'."

"What in the world is 'second sight'?" I asked.

"Well, to give you an example, she said at breakfast this morning that she would probably see her next husband today or tomorrow!"

"Who's he to be?" I asked, now completely hooked.

"I don't know, but what spooks me the most is that Hester told me, on the way in, that she believes her. I'll tell you, Will, I'm getting too old for this. I've had thirty years of staying on my toes with Hester, and I don't know if I'm ready for another challenge at my age!"

"Look at it this way, Jess, if she's right about seeing her next husband, maybe she won't be around that long."

"Will, have you ever been around a woman who's set her hat for some poor man?"

"Not for a while, at least," I admitted.

"It ain't a pretty thing," Jess mused, as he turned to join Hester.

Effie Johansson was an attractive woman, who appeared to be in her mid to late thirties, about Jacob's age. As that thought crossed my mind, two things happened: the hair on the back of my neck stood straight, and I looked around quickly, to see if I could spot Jacob. He had been coming to services ever since he'd been appointed marshal. He said he thought it was "proper and fitting." To this day, Jacob Webber in a chapel has always caused two emotions in my mind: humor and fear. Humor at the thought of some of his arsenal falling out of their hiding places while he is in the chapel and fear of the same possibility.

Why I had thought to look for Jacob at the prospect of Effie Johansson seeing her new husband seemed a little strange. But nevertheless, I had a strong temptation to send Jacob back to the ranch and tell him to stay there, at least for the next several days.

On the way home after church, Clatilda asked me if I had met Effie. I told her that Jess and Hester had introduced me to their niece.

"How do you like her?" I asked.

"Well, I think she is very nice, and you will get to know her better tomorrow. She and Hester are coming out to spend the day."

"Tomorrow?"

"Yes. Is that a problem?"

"All day Monday?" I again asked.

"Will, what's wrong?" Clatilda asked, turning in her seat to face me.

"Oh, well, it's dumb, but I might as well tell you."

I then told her all, from Effie's supposed 'second sight' to my thoughts about Jacob.

When I had finished, Clatilda clapped her hands in delight, not unlike a child on Christmas morning.

"Oh, Will, wouldn't it be wonderful for our Jacob to finally have his own family?"

"Ma'am, is there something deep inside a woman that simply cannot stand to see a single man?"

"You've been so mistreated as a married man?"

"No, but you know what I mean." I said, now looking for a way out of the hole I had dug for myself.

"Of course I do, Will Jackson. And I also know that you're right. It's against nature for a man to wander around, hungry, shirttail hanging out and always in trouble. It's up to us women to change all that."

"Do women talk about this crusade when they're together?"

"Of course, cowboy, when do you think we make our plans?"

I quickly looked at her, and that hussy just winked at me.

"Poor, poor Jacob," was all I could think.

Monday morning dawned bright and clear. Cool, but a nice spring day.

Jacob announced at breakfast that he and Jim Ballard would be close that day as they intended to rebuild part of the corral fencing. My impulse was to suggest he go into town to check on the work at the hotel. But he squelched that thought by saying the work on the hotel was stable as there would only be four men working this week, as most had other chores at their homes. I wished for a way to keep him out of sight. But then, I drew myself up short. Surely, I wasn't buying into this 'second sight' malarkey.

Monday morning found J.W. and I back in my office working on the dockets for Alamosa and Trinidad and researching the answer to an argument we I had been having over a part of my handling of the Mayhugh situation in Trinidad. I was still uneasy and J.W. kept insisting there was precedent for what I had done.

We'd not been long at out efforts, when I heard a commotion in the front of the house and I knew our guests had arrived. I didn't want to go out there, but I felt I probably should.

Cowardice won out, and J.W. and I stayed in my office.

It was only moments, however, before the three women invaded our hideout.

"Will Jackson, what do you mean hiding back here?" Hester said as she came into the room. "Don't you know I want to hear all about you're being a judge? And, I want you to get to know my niece. Did you meet Effie at church yesterday?"

"Yes ma'am," I said, standing.

"Well, come on out here. Clatilda can make us some hot chocolate and we can talk!"

J.W. quietly told me he would continue to read. I whispered to him, as I left, about what a sneaky coward I considered him to be. He just smiled and turned back to his table of books.

When we were seated in the dining room, Hester opened the serious conversation.

"Will, I'm showing Effie around the area so she can meet as many folks as possible."

"That's nice," I answered.

"Yes, she needs to see as many folks as she can, because yesterday or today she will see the man who is to be her next husband!"

I came that close to spilling a cup of hot chocolate on Clatilda's good tablecloth.

"Do you suppose she will know him when she sees him?" I asked of no one in particular.

"Mr. Jackson," Mrs. Johansson spoke up, "I'm right here. If you have a question of me, I will be happy to answer."

All of a sudden, I was real anxious to be somewhere else. Anywhere else.

"Mrs. Johansson, I didn't intend to be rude. It's just that this conversation is a little off my range."

"That's all right, sir. I have noticed that most men become very uncomfortable when women go husband-hunting. And it doesn't seem to matter whether they are the object of such a hunt or just an innocent bystander."

"Jacob," I thought, "you don't have a chance."

I looked around that table at which I had known many a happy time. Everyone of those women was looking back at me without any expression on their faces at all.

There have been times in my life when I was in immediate danger of serious injury or death. I was never so scared and uncertain as, at that moment. I excused myself and went back to my office where I carefully closed and locked the door.

J.W. looked up when he heard the lock turn.

"Is there a problem, Will?"

"Yeah, J.W., there are three women out there."

"Sir?"

"J.W., there are three of God's most dangerous creatures sitting not forty feet from where I'm standing."

J.W. looked at me as if I'd taken leave of my senses. He was absolutely right!

We continued to work until just after noon when Clatilda knocked on the door and called out that dinner was ready.

It didn't dawn on me until later that she had not even tried the door. It was as if she had known it to be locked.

Dinner was pleasant. I dreaded for Jacob to meet Effie, but the introductions were handled by each in a totally off-handed manner.

I was not until Jacob was excusing himself to return to his work that the other shoe hit the floor.

"Mr. Webber," Effie spoke up, "Wednesday evening, I will have a fresh beef stew, raisin pie and hot cornbread ready at about seven, at my aunt's home. I would appreciate it if you would be on time."

Her statement stopped Jacob in his tracks, much as if he had walked into a wall.

Most everyone knew of Jacob's love of beef stew and cornbread but, outside my family, I would have bet no one knew that Jacob would walk ten miles, barefoot, for even a small slice of raisin pie.

I looked over at Clatilda, and for one of the very few times in our lives, I saw a look of wonder on her face.

"Ma'am, I'm not right sure I'll be able to make that. My work sometimes runs late," Jacob finally stuttered.

"Oh, I'm sure Mr. Jackson will let you quit early that evening. Won't you, Mr. Jackson?" Effie said, turning to look straight at me.

I couldn't help it. Jacob was like a brother to me, but I looked right at him and said, "Of course, Mrs. Johansson, I'm sure Jacob could even quit at noon to give himself plenty of time."

Jacob looked at me, as one whose betrayal was as complete as that of Judas.

"Yes, ma'am," he stammered, "I'll be on time."

"There now you see, Mr. Webber, it 's all settled. I'll see you at seven the day after tomorrow."

The whole day was a let-down, after dinner. Hester and Effie left about mid-afternoon. After the goodbyes were over, I went in to the kitchen to see Clatilda.

"Do you believe what went on at dinner?" I asked.

"The one thing I do believe is that you better decide where you're going to build Jacob's house."

"You don't really believe in that 'second sight' stuff, do you?"

"What I do believe is that Effie Johansson has set her sights on Jacob, and the lady strikes me as one very determined individual."

Right then, I had the strangest feeling. It was not unlike being in a fist fight. After the first two or three blows, the anticipation and dread are over. What happens then can never be worse than the anticipation. I felt Jacob to be in good hands, and what was to be, would be.

Chapter 13

Real winter set in the Wednesday after Thanksgiving that year. Snowstorm followed snowstorm, relentlessly piling up. By mid-December there was over three feet of snow on the level. Drifts varied, but many were several feet deep. It required everyone's best efforts to tend the herd. Even J.W. turned out to help.

Seth and his boys also helped out. In addition to caring for the livestock, we had need of more firewood than we'd put up. Jim Ballard's wife was having trouble getting over the difficult birth of her second child, and Clatilda insisted their home be kept as warm as a summer afternoon.

We spent some long cold days cutting dead timber, east of the Blalock place. But, by the middle of December, we had established a good routine and had a pile of split firewood that was fast taking on the proportions of a good-sized house.

I knew when our wood-cutting days were over. One morning at breakfast, Clatilda asked me what I had planned that day.

"We've got to move some of the herd over to the west end, then after that, we'll probably go for more wood."

"Why don't you let Jim and Uncle Buck move that herd. Hester Turner send word inviting us over for a visit. I was thinking maybe you, Jacob and I might just go visiting today."

"Are you sure?" I asked.

"Why, yes. Don't you want to go?" she asked.

"Well, yeah. But there are still three or four trees left on that mountain behind Seth's. I thought we were going to clear-cut that hill."

"Keep it up, cowboy! The next cobbler I fix you, you'll have to gum. You'll be so old, you won't have any teeth left!"

The wood cutting was over, and we went visiting.

The children did not even try to get to school during December and January. Little Jake had his first pony and Bud's old saddle, and he tried his best to help also.

Christmas that year was interesting. We had the Turners over, along with Effie Johansson and, of course, the Blalocks.

Jacob and Effie were still sparring. That is to say, Jacob was. Effie seemed quite comfortable. Why not? She had set the hook and was now just playing Jacob before reeling him in.

Jess Turner's health had begun to fail somewhat, and I had, twice, after the weather worsened sent Jacob and Bud over to lend a hand with his chores. He had few, as he no longer kept much stock, just enough to care for his and Hester's needs. He blustered somewhat about Jacob and Bud's help, but Hester said they were both grateful.

Bud told us later that Mrs. Johansson was almost as good on a horse as Clatilda, and some stronger. He said he could tell Jacob was impressed, not openly, but impressed, nonetheless.

We all wondered if there would be an exchange of gifts between Jacob and Effie. None, however, would have guessed the real situation.

We all opened our gifts on Christmas Eve. There was never anything elaborate, but always some solid remembrance for everyone. Clatilda gave me a new satchel, and we both gave J.W. a new grip. It was one of the new Gladstones everyone seemed to carrying at least most of the attorneys on my circuit. He seemed right pleased.

We all watched as Effie opened her gift from Jacob. We were shocked to see it was one of those new bolt action rifles. Effie was not. She seemed genuinely pleased. But when Jacob opened his, I began seriously considering where we might build his house. Effie gave him a matched set of the finest looking colt revolvers I'd ever seen. They were complete with real bone handle grips.

Clatilda cornered me after the gift giving was over.

"Will, do you think the gift Jacob gave Effie was appropriate?"

"She seemed pleased."

"Yes, but a rifle? That's the kind of gift I'd give you or Bud. I'd not expect to get one from you!"

"Do you know if she owns one?"

"No. I do know Hester said she carried a derringer in her purse. Hester said she carries it always."

"Well, I don't think you have to worry about her owning a rifle like Jacob gave her. I've only seen a few. They're not made for quick action. They're more for hunting and long-range shooting. I was reading about them in John's store a month or so ago. According to the pamphlet, they can be accurate up to five hundred yards. Don't you know, that's over a quarter of a mile!"

"How far is your Winchester accurate?" she asked.

"I personally have never been sure of any shot over two hundred yards. I've heard those who claimed to have hit their targets at up to three or even four hundred yards with a Winchester. I've, personally, never seen such shots, and frankly doubt they've been made with a Winchester."

"I must admit, the wood on the rifle's stock is beautiful. But a rifle as a gift for a woman?"

"Not just any woman. Somehow the gift seems about right for both the giver and the receiver," I said.

"It worries me that she might be like Jacob. They could start their own army!" I added.

"Will, if there was any question about her feelings for Jacob, those Colt pistols should answer it. I saw John at the store last week and he showed me the invoice. He ordered them for Effie specifically as she described them. I was told her husband had left her comfortable. But, Will, she's more than just comfortable, and our Jacob is in for it, if that gift is any indication. John wanted to know if they would be married in the church. Has Jacob said anything to you?"

"No, and I'll not ask. That's something that's his and Effie's business. We should stay out of it."

"Oh, men!" Clatilda said and went about her business in the kitchen.

Christmas day dawned clear, cold and bright.

Shortly after breakfast, I heard shots out behind the old barn. I got my hat and asked Uncle Buck to come with me to find the source of the shooting.

"I don't think I would, Pa," Bud spoke up. "Mr. Webber and Mrs. Johansson are trying out their new guns."

I looked in the kitchen to see Clatilda, Hester and Anne Blalock all looking at me with sweet smiles on their faces.

"Poor Jacob," I thought. But then I thought, "Why poor? She's a good woman, and Jacob must be loved."

January continued as December-cold, raw, and much snow and ice. In January, I received a letter from Jamie Nava. He said he had a serious problem and wanted me to hold a special court session in Alamosa. He gave me few details but said the situation was serious and an early trial would probably be the only way to defuse the situation.

Due to the weather and the road and trail conditions, Clatilda stayed at home and J.W. and I went horseback.

We rode into Alamosa in the midst of a howling blizzard. We'd made the last thirty miles by J.W.'s compass and a few landmarks. When we had stabled our horses and went into the hotel, the desk clerk, upon seeing my name on the register told me Jamie wanted to see me as soon as I arrived. As it was almost ten at night, I suggested we'd see him in the morning. The clerk disputed that, saying Jamie had left word to be notified of our arrival, even should we get in after midnight.

I had hardly gotten settled in my room when there came a rap on my door. I opened it to find Jamie.

"Will, thank you for coming so quickly," was his greeting as he stepped into the room.

"Well, your letter was such that dawdling was not a choice."

"I've got trouble, Will. The kind of trouble that could tear this country wide open."

"Sit down. Let's start at the beginning."

"I don't know how much we should go over the details, Will. I have three people under arrest. Two I've charged with murder and the other with the attempted murder of two women."

"Those are serious charges, Jamie. Have you evidence to support them?"

"Oh yes, Will. All incidents occurred inside the courthouse before at least fifty eyewitnesses."

"With such an airtight case, Jamie, why the urgency to hold the trial?"

"The two murdered men are members of one of the biggest families in the valley, and the two women wounded by the third man are members of the family of the two men I've charged with murder. These two men and the two wounded women are members of the family holding the largest ranch in the valley."

"Jamie, how did such a situation come to be?"

"It's involved, Will, and I'm not sure just how much detail I should give, in that you are to be the trial judge in the murder trial."

"Well, I believe I should be allowed, at least, to know the history of whatever brought all this about. That is, the general complaints, if not the individuals' contributions to the situations."

"That I can do! The Stewarts came into the valley about ten years ago. I believe they came from Virginia or North Carolina. Somehow, they'd made it through the war with some money left, unusual for anyone from the South. But as soon as they hit this valley, they began to buy up land. They only bought that with a provable clear title. They were right careful about that. When it all settled out, they owned an awful lot of country. Mostly in the eastern end of the valley. Everything from some fairly useless desert, to fine timberland, and just about everything in between. Old man Stewart had five boys and two daughters. The girls are pretty as pictures, and the boys mean as peach orchard boars. It was these two girls who were shot. Two of the boys are the ones I'm holding for murder."

"What in the world brought all this about?" I asked.

"I'm getting to that. After old man Stewart got his ranch all rounded-up, he put out the word he would not tolerate trespassing.

Anyone could ask, and maybe receive permission, to cross or be on his land, for any legitimate purpose, but trespassers would be shot. This was when I was sheriff, and as some of his land was in my jurisdiction, I rode out to suggest his off-hand shooting of trespassers might be the wrong approach. He told me right quick that he meant what he said, and if it ever came to a shooting in my county, we'd talk about it, but until then, the warning stood.

"There were several incidents over the years, but no shootings. A couple of times the Stewart boys roughed up a couple of people but usually with provable cause, if not total justification."

Last fall, in October, four of the Padilla boys went upon the mountains northeast of here to cut firewood. They had done this all their lives. They had to cross a corner of the Stewart ranch to get where they wanted to cut wood. Now, they had been doing this for all the time Stewart had owned that land at least ten years. That morning all of the Stewarts clan, including their ranch foremen and several hands were moving cattle down out of their summer graze. The two groups met each other on a creek. Old man Stewart ordered the Padilla boys off his ranch. The Padillas say they tried to talk to him, but they were pulled out of their wagons by the Stewart boys and severely beaten. One of the Padilla boys Ernesto, is still in bed. The Stewarts then piled the Padillas back in their wagon led the team to the edge of the Stewart property and left them. They were found there, later that afternoon, by a rancher from up by Mosca. He knew the boys and took them home.

Old Theodoro Padilla came to see me about it. I met old man Stewart and two of his boys the next morning coming into the courthouse. He readily admitted to the beating and told me the Padillas should be glad he had not shot them. I told him that if the Padillas pressed charges, I'd have to send Sheriff Hatcher to arrest him and those of his boys who were involved. He said if that happened, I should tell Hatcher to come riding a good horse and packing a bag full of grub. Because he would be in for a long trip.

"As it turned out, the Padillas did file charges and I did have to send Sheriff Hatcher to arrest three of the Stewarts and two of their cowboys. You know Hatcher, Will. He didn't even take a full canteen."

"He just rode out to the ranch, arrested the old man, put him in irons and brought him in to Alamosa. The whole clan arrived within four hours. Hatcher then sorted out the three boys and the two cowboys, then he released the old man."

"We held the trial in early November, and I sentenced the three Stewart boys and their ranch hands to ninety days in the county jail. As everyone was leaving the courtroom, two of the Stewart boys I now have in jail, confronted the two Padillas who had testified against them. Neither of the Padillas was armed. The Stewarts shot both the Padilla boys at point blank range. The other Padilla boy, Julio, who was at the original fracas, drew and fired. He says he was firing at the Stewart boys who shot his brothers, but he hit the two Stewart girls instead. I had no choice but to lock him up and charge him along with the Stewart boys. Luckily, the girls will live."

"Will, this whole valley is like an armed camp. The Padillas have, literally, hundreds of bloodline relatives in this area, and most of the Anglo ranchers and even some townspeople have sided with the Stewarts. We need to settle this thing, and right now. I think a speedy trial would at least begin the quieting process."

"Have you thought that a guilty verdict, all around, might just blow the top off the whole mess?"

"Yes, and that also scares me."

"Jamie, is there any reason to believe a jury might not convict any one of the three people you have jailed?"

"You know juries as well as I do, Will. Anything can happen."

"Will it be possible to seat a jury that has no Padilla relatives or those sympathetic to the rancher's cause?"

"Possible, maybe. But, I would have to say, not likely."

"Do you suppose the three would agree to a trial by judge?"

"Afraid not, Will."

"All right, you have presented me with a problem that has only one solution. Who's your prosecutor?"

"I'd thought to have you appoint one of the attorneys traveling with your circuit."

"What would you say if I have him ask for a change of venue to Trinidad?"

"Won't work."

"Why not?"

"The Padillas have already thought of that, and their threats are even more serious in that event."

"You've got a real tiger by the tail, haven't you, Jamie?"

"Yeah, and I don't see it getting much better, regardless of what's done."

"All right, then. Let's just go ahead with the trials. In all honesty, given the facts you've presented, I don't see anything getting a lot better. When do you want to start?"

"Well, I know two of your attorneys are here in town, working on other matters. Mr. Fisher came with you, I suppose?"

"Yes, he's in the room next door."

"How does day after tomorrow suit you?"

"Let's do it."

The next morning I checked at the hotel desk, and was pleased to find Abel Tyson to be one of the attorneys in town. I found him in the hotel café.

I spoke to him and was invited to join him for breakfast.

I had no more than seated myself when he spoke up.

"I know what you're going to ask. I would like to decline, but I don't see how I can, do you?"

"Frankly, I'm no more pleased to be trying the case, than you will be to prosecute. I see it as one of those things where no one wins. Do you know who the Stewarts and the Padillas will have representing them?"

"Yes, the old man Padilla grabbed hold of John Tyler as soon as we hit town. He and I had come up from Trinidad to clear up some civil matters we had here and to be here when you came in the first of the month. It seems Tyler had done some work previously for the Padillas. As for the Stewarts, I don't know."

"Have you any problems starting the trial tomorrow?" I asked.

"I must have heard the story a hundred times in the last ten days. Everyone tells the same set of facts. I suspect the litigation side of this problem to be pretty straightforward. It's after you pass the sentences that the party begins. And, by the way, which trial comes first? That's a bit of timing that, to me, seems most critical."

"I know. I've been studying on that, and I may have found a way to defuse the timing problem. I will try the capital case against the Stewarts and have Jamie Nava try the case against the Padilla boy at the same time. I think that could put a couple of issues to bed."

"That's good thinking! As a matter of fact, that may be the best, if not the only, way to begin to quiet this whole thing."

"I think so. In fact, after I talked to you, I'd planned to present the matter to Jamie."

"Whatever happens, should I be prepared to proceed against the two Stewarts tomorrow morning?"

"Plan on it. The only thing that would foul things up could be the Stewarts' attorney. I shouldn't think they would not be able to afford one. At any rate, you go ahead. Your preparations won't be wasted, anyway. I'll let you know by noon today if there's any problem with tomorrow morning. You go ahead and get with Sheriff Hatcher. He can line up your witnesses for you."

I left Mr. Tyson at his breakfast and set out to find Jamie. I found him in his office.

When I presented my plan to Jamie, he leaned back in his chair and stared out the window of his office for a few moments.

"Will, I believe you may have hit on the only possible way to put an end to this issue. For Jamie Nava to preside over the trial of Julio Padilla and Will Jackson to preside over the trial of Len and Buck Stewart will make it pretty tough for anyone to claim favoritism. Now, if we can just first get a couple of decent juries."

"Jamie, can you be ready to begin the trial of the Padilla boy tomorrow?"

"Only if I can find someone to prosecute."

"Have you no local attorneys that can be pressed into service?"

"Well, there's C. J. Henderson. He's young and has only been here for a few months."

"He'll have to do. Can you see him this morning?"

"I'll get it done, Will."

I stood to leave his office.

"Will, thanks for your help on this one. I am still nervous but I believe your idea will go far towards solving a problem that could have gotten real ugly."

"Jamie, if I have helped, maybe it will be a small token toward my long-standing debt to you. Let's just hope we can get out of this thing without more killings."

"Will, if it gets bad, have you the authority to bring in the state militia?"

"No, I don't. But I have the right to request the governor to do so. But, frankly, Jamie, after some of the things done by our state militia the past few years, I think the governor might be a little gun-shy. But if we have the kind of situation develop here, that seems possible, I don't see how he could refuse."

Chapter 14

Len and Buck Stewart, indeed, had an attorney. I found he had in fact been a guest at the Stewart ranch for a few weeks. That must have put a dent in the Senior Stewart's bankroll. The attorney was one Hiram Goodpasture, of the firm of Goodpasture, Davis, and Latrell of Denver. I'd heard of both Mr. Goodpasture and his firm. Two things stood out about their reputation: they were good and they were expensive. Some just said, good and expensive.

I was amused to see Goodpasture as he walked into my courtroom. He was dressed from head to toe in what, I guess, he considered a rancher's costume. Brand new Stetson and brand new riding boots. And brand new everything in-between. First, I grinned, then I thought of what fools he must think we, who dressed as he did, to be. It was at that moment that I lost respect for Mr. Goodpasture, no matter how good and expensive he might be.

When the deputy brought the Stewart boys into the courtroom, I was shocked at their apparent young ages. I had heard everyone calling them "boys," but I just thought this to be a form of separating them from old man Stewart. Neither of them could have been much over seventeen, maybe eighteen.

After J.W. read the charges, I asked for the Stewarts' plea. Both pled "not guilty." I asked Goodpasture if he was ready, to which he responded with the beginning of a tirade about the injustice of the trial. I stopped him by rapping my gavel over and saying simply "shut up, counselor."

Mr. Goodpasture almost sat on his brand-new Stetson. I suppose he was seldom issued such an order.

We spent the entire day selecting a jury. When the twelve were seated along with two alternates, neither Tyson nor Goodpasture was very happy with the panel. That fact, alone, told me we probably had the best jury possible.

It was early in the morning of the second day of the trial before opening statements were given by the two attorneys. Tyson, as prosecutor, said simply that he had enough eye witnesses to prove the Stewarts had shot and killed Juan and Celestino Padilla, even though both Padillas had been unarmed.

Goodpasture started by asking for a change of venue, which I denied. He then moved for a dismissal of charges. I refused. He then told the jury that he would show the Stewarts had only reacted to aggressive moves by the Padillas. In fact, he said, had not the Padillas acted as they did, the Stewarts would not have been forced to defend themselves.

Tyson began with his witnesses. I could tell he and Sheriff Hatcher had been busy. Before noon of the second day of the trial, Tyson had presented nine witnesses. They all told the same story. Len and Buck Stewart had walked up to the two Padilla boys, drawn their pistols and shot both Padillas, at point-blank range. Not one of the witnesses had heard either the Stewarts or the Padillas say a word.

After Tyson's ninth witness had testified, Tyson turned to me and said, "Judge Jackson, I have many more witnesses who all have the same testimony to offer. But, in the interest of expediting this matter, should I continue?"

"It's your case, Mr. Tyson," I responded.

He stood for a moment, then turning to face Goodpasture and the Stewart boys, he said. "The prosecution moves for an immediate, directed verdict of guilty."

"I'm sorry, Counselor, I cannot do so without giving the accused a chance to present their case. Motion denied."

"Very well, your honor," Tyson said and called his tenth witness.

Goodpasture leaned back in his chair, "Your honor, given the hour, could we not take a noon recess before Mr. Tyson goes on with his harangue?"

"No," I said.

"But, sir, it is already half past twelve. Surely there is nothing to be gained by postponing the noon break another half-hour or forty-five minutes."

"Mr. Goodpasture, one of the few privileges I enjoy is deciding when or if I wish to adjourn the proceedings in my courtroom. We will not adjourn at this time."

"Well, then, would your honor mind if I sent out for sandwiches for me and my clients?"

"You may send out for whatever you please, sir. But, this is neither a café, or saloon. If I find anyone eating or drinking in my courtroom, I will give them ten days in Mr. Hatcher's jail to consider the error of their ways."

"But, your honor!" Goodpasture said, half standing up from his chair.

"Sit down, Mr. Goodpasture! And shut up!"

"I will not be spoken to like that, sir. I'm not some hick lawyer like Wilton Mayhugh!"

The room fell silent immediately. I then realized how far the story of my treatment of Wilton Mayhugh had traveled.

"Mr. Goodpasture, I am going to take the time of the court to explain a couple of things to you. You may be some punkins where you come from. You may even be able to bully judges, in their own courtroom. But, let me tell you something, sir; and I will say this only once. While you are in my courtroom you will do as I say! Or, sir, you will find yourself no longer in my courtroom. One other thing I noticed: you have a pistol under your coat. I've also noticed others in the room who are armed. Sheriff Hatcher and his deputy will go among you, and you will surrender all firearms to him. Anyone who wishes, may retain your weapons, but they will then leave the courtroom."

There was quite a bit of grumbling, but only two men left the crowded room. Goodpasture started, once again, to make an issue of my directive but decided against it.

We did not recess for dinner. Tyson continued through the afternoon, interviewing one witness after another. Goodpasture's cross-examinations were brief and seemed to follow no pattern.

At six, that evening, I adjourned the proceedings until eight the next morning. I was anxious to talk to Jamie to see how his trial was going. We met for supper in his home.

"Will," Jamie said, as soon as we were seated at his table, "I don't see how I am going to be able to do anything but throw the book at Julio. The girls were far enough to the side of their brothers that Julio would have to be a lot worse shot than I know him to be, to have been so far off."

"Do you think he shot the girls on purpose?"

"I just don't know. But, I've got a hunch he just shot the first Stewarts he saw. More's the pity they had to be the girls."

"Were any other Stewarts near the girls?"

"No one except the old man, who was standing…"

Jamie stopped and seemed to be looking into space.

"Of course!" Jamie said, slapping his hand on the table. "Old man Stewart was just behind and a little to the side of the girls."

"Then you have a problem, Jamie."

"I do, and no way out of it. Will, this is so much like the first case you tried in my court. The one where that miner shot the young man and his girl friend."

"I remember, but, like you said, you are cornered. You can't discuss your thoughts with either the prosecutor or defense council."

"No, I'll just have to see how it unfolds. How's your trial going?"

I related the day's events to him.

"I wish I'd been there. I saw Goodpasture come into the courthouse this morning. He was sure dressed up, wasn't he?"

"Yes, but Jamie, I've seen no one I could identify as the Stewart family. I asked Sheriff Hatcher, and he said he'd seen the whole clan earlier but he agreed; they were not in my courtroom."

"Good reason, too. They are all in mine. Every last one of them."

"Were they armed?"

"You know, I didn't notice. I'll look closer tomorrow. Like you, I don't care for a bunch of pistol-toting cowboys in my courtroom."

"Why do you suppose they were at your trial, instead of the one involving their sons or brothers?"

"Does seem strange."

I was surprised, the next morning at the crowd I found in my courtroom, at eight. I'd expected much fewer.

Tyson continued with his parade of eye-witnesses. I was amazed at how closely their testimonies stuck to the same few facts, with very little difference in what they said.

Again, I did not recess at noon. Tyson rested his case a little after four, that afternoon.

I asked Goodpasture if he was ready to present his defense.

"I am, your honor, but due to the lateness, might I suggest we start tomorrow morning?"

"No."

"No? But, your honor, it's after four!"

"If you're ready, get on with it; if not, just say so!"

Goodpasture looked at me for a moment and seemed to be on the verge of saying more, but turned to a man sitting just behind one of the Stewarts. He said something to the man, who then hurried out of the courtroom.

Goodpasture then stood and called Len Stewart to the stand.

Goodpasture immediately began having Len tell of the incident at the creek where he and the others had beaten the Padillas.

Tyson objected to this line of questioning as not being relevant.

Goodpasture said he was trying to show why Len and Buck Stewart were afraid of the Padillas.

I allowed the line of questioning to continue.

Goodpasture went on to have Len explain that they were afraid of what the Padillas might do, and that was why the Stewarts were armed, that day, in the hallway of the courthouse. Len went on to say that when he and his brother had confronted the Padillas, they had thought the Padillas to be armed.

Goodpasture then turned Len over to Tyson for cross-examination.

Tyson walked right up, and stood just in front of Len.

"I have just three questions of you, Mr. Stewart. First, did you shoot one of the Padilla boys?"

"Yes sir."

"Did you shoot both the Padillas?"

"No sir."

"Did you see any firearms on the person of either of the Padillas, whom you confronted?"

"No, sir, but they could have had a 'hide-out'."

"No further questions," Tyson said, turning his back on Stewart, and walking to his table.

We went through exactly the same routine with Buck Stewart. By the time Tyson was through with Buck, it was a little after six. So, I adjourned the court until eight the next morning.

Jamie and I, once again, had supper at his house. He told me he had shut down a little before three that afternoon and would be ready, the next morning, for summations by both attorneys. I asked him how he thought it was going.

"Will, it has always been an open and shut case. I can't see the jury returning with any other than a guilty verdict."

"I think that's the way mine is going also. Now comes the rough part. The sentencing is where the lid could blow off."

"Well, I've some leeway. For attempted murder, I can sentence from ten years to life. I think if I were to give him ten years, I'd probably have some pretty angry people."

"I hate to think about my case. I'd like to think I could hand down some Solomon-like ruling, but so far, the case is too cut and dried for that. I'm going to have to wait and see what the jury says."

Summations the next morning were mercifully short and to the point. Tyson told the jury any verdict short of murder, in the first degree, would be a mockery, and Goodpasture hit hard on the probable self-defense angle.

The jury was out about fifteen minutes. When they came back in to announce their verdict, they interrupted my quiet prayers about the sentencing.

What I had been thinking was whether it would be better to send them to the state penitentiary at Canon City to be hung, or to hang them in Alamosa.

The jury lined in and took their seats. I asked the jury foreman if they had reached a verdict.

"We have, sir."

"How do you find in the case against John Leonard Steward?"

"We find him guilty of murder, in the first degree"

There was a ripple went through the spectators, which I stopped with a rap of my gavel.

"How do you find in the case of Jason Roebuck Stewart?"

"We find him guilty of murder, in the first degree"

I sat for a moment, knowing that the passing of sentence was expected and usual.

"This court will stand adjourned, until two this afternoon, at which time I will sentence the defendants."

I whispered to J.W. that I was going to my room at the hotel and not to disturb me unless something very important came up.

I went there for two reasons. One, I wanted some quiet time to myself, so that I might finish my prayer, interrupted by the jury's return, and secondly, to check on a thought that had been nagging, at the back of my mind.

It was a little after one-thirty when Jamie knocked on my door and identified himself.

Without preamble, after he had entered, he advised me of the mood of some of the conversations he had overheard.

"Will, many are saying that if you try to send the Stewarts to Canon City for hanging, they'll never get there, and if you try to hang them here, we'll never get the gallows built."

"Doesn't look good, does it, my friend?"

"No, Will, and I am sorry to have brought you into this mess."

"Jamie, I don't remember anyone promising me an easy job. In fact, I believe I remember telling myself just the opposite. So, your trial's complete?"

"Yes, I've already sentenced Julio Padilla to twelve years at Canon City."

"Then, why don't you come with me when I pronounce sentence on the Stewarts. I would appreciate your company."

"It's the least I can do."

As Jamie and I walked back to the courthouse, we passed several groups of men standing around. They seemed to fall in behind us, as if by signal. By the time I reached my bench, the courtroom was full, to overflowing out into the hall.

When I was seated, I told the defendants to rise.

"Gentlemen," I began, after they and Goodpasture were standing, "have you anything you would like to say before I pass sentence?"

"Yeah, I have," spoke up Buck Stewart. "I ain't ashamed of what we did. I still say those Padilla's were getting ready to jump us. But, judge, you ain't going to hang me, and my brother; here or down at the 'pen.' My pa won't let that happen."

To Goodpasture's credit he tried to quiet the young man. Even to practically pushing him down in his chair.

"Counselor, please let your client alone. I want him standing when I pass sentence. I want him and his brother to understand a few things. I suspect it will be wise if even his family pays close attention to what I say. In fact what I have to say now is to all the Stewart's and to those who might think to support them in what they do. If I choose to hang you young men, I have the choice of hanging you right here in Alamosa or having you hung at the territory penitentiary, in Canon City. Also, should anyone interfere with either your hanging, here in Alamosa, or your transport to Canon City, it is within my power to punish those persons also. And believe me, should that come to pass, this country will not soon forget what happens then. For, understand me, I'll not just press Sheriff Hatcher into the action, although I believe him quite capable, but, gentlemen, understand me! If there is any attempted interference in the judgement I hand down against these young men, I will immediately declare that an edict of martial law should exist in this entire valley and have the governor send however many of the state's militia I believe will be necessary to enforce that law. If you have any doubts of my ability to do this, ask your Mr. Goodpasture. If any of you believe I'll not do as I say, again, ask Mr. Goodpasture.

"I will not tolerate any violent reaction to whatever this, or any court in this court's jurisdiction, may hand down to any convicted felon. Is that perfectly understood by all present?"

I waited for a long count of twenty before proceeding. During which time you could have heard a pen drop in that room.

"All right, young men, I am not going to hang you."

I paused, expecting some sort of vocal reaction from the spectators. At least from the Stewart clan. None was forthcoming.

"Very well, then. What you young men did is absolutely unforgivable, and unjustifiable. While I am not going to hang you, I am, all the same, going to take your life, as you have known it. You and your attorney chose to have you tried together, rather than separately. Therefore, in the eyes of this court you have, each, been convicted of killing both the Padillas. I will then, sentence each of you for two killings. John Leonard Stewart, I sentence you to one hundred years in the territory prison for the murder of Juan Padilla. I further sentence you to one hundred years in the territory prison for the murder of Celestino Padilla. That is to say; each of you is, in fact, sentenced to two hundred years

Without waiting for any reaction, I turned to Buck Stewart.

"Well, sir! Jason Roebuck Stewart, I sentence you to one hundred years in the state prison for the murder of Juan Padilla and one hundred years in the state prison for the murder of Celestino Padilla. I furthermore rule that these sentences shall run consecutively. Not, and I repeat, not, concurrently.

"Now, young men, I am told the state authorities have begun giving time off, up to one third of a sentence, for good behavior. This means you could serve as little as one hundred and thirty or thirty-five years."

"Now, Mr. Goodpasture you pay close attention to what I say now."

I turned to J.W. "And, Mr. Fisher, please see that you get every single word I am about to say. I want there to be no misunderstanding later."

"Mr. Goodpasture, you and I both know you have the right to appeal my decision and, in fact, this entire case. In which event, the appellate court will either throw out the entire conviction, which is probably very unlikely, or they will send the case back to this court for retrial."

"Now, Mr. Goodpasture, understand me well, if ever again I hear a case in this immediate area, where such cold blooded murder is committed, I promise you I will have the guilty parties hanged. And right here in Alamosa's town square. Do you understand exactly what I am saying?"

I paused, but there was not a sound in the room.

"Mr. Goodpasture, I asked you, sir, if you understood what I said. I expect an answer, and right now!"

Goodpasture looked at me for a moment, then ducking his head, mumbled something.

"Mr. Goodpasture, I did not hear you, sir."

"Yes, dammit, I understand!" Goodpasture practically shouted.

I waited a moment, then turned to Sheriff Hatcher.

"Sheriff, will it be convenient for you to transport these two men to Canon City the day after tomorrow?"

"Yes, your honor," Hatcher responded.

"Good. Then, Mr. Hatcher, I would that you allow the Stewart family free access to these young men tomorrow, in their cells. Their family may visit them from sunup until sundown. Have you a cell large enough to accommodate such a gathering?"

"Yes, sir," Hatcher said.

"Therefore, then, this court is adjourned."

Chapter 15

J.W. and I stayed on in Alamosa for four days after the end of the Stewart trial. We cleared the docket and started home the morning of the fifth day to spend a couple of weeks before the beginning of court in Trinidad.

On our ride back to the ranch, we discussed the Stewart trial.

"Will, if Goodpasture appeals the case, he could do so by saying you threatened him that he should not."

"I don't think so, J.W.. But, if he does, so be it. I believe I can justify anything I said. And, if an appellate court reverses the case, they will have to send it back to me or another judge at my level. Frankly, I doubt any other judge would be as lenient as I."

It was long after dark when we rode into the ranch yard and cold, cold. I had teased J.W. for the last few hours about the warm bed he could be in if he'd stayed in Alamosa. His responses had generally been about how poorly café food compared to Clatilda's.

I was surprised for the last couple of miles to see the ranch lit up like a small town. There were even lanterns hung outside.

As we drew closer, I could see much activity.

We rode into the yard to be welcomed by my family, Jim Ballard, his wife, the entire Blalock clan and Uncle Buck. In addition Jess and Hester Turner were also there. I also saw Effie Johansson through the door, in our kitchen.

"What in the world is going on here?" I demanded of Clatilda, as she came to greet us.

"Oh, Will, I'm so glad you made it back. We're having an engagement party for Jacob and Effie day after tomorrow night. We sent word to you. Is that why you're back so soon?"

"I received no word. We just finished our business in Alamosa and came home. What's this about an engagement party?"

"Yes, Will, isn't it great? Jacob and Effie have decided to marry in the spring."

"Why the wait?"

"Jacob insists he will have a home for his wife, and he says it will take that long to get it built."

"Can't Uncle Buck move in with us and Jacob and Effie take the cabin?"

"Uncle Buck offered, even to move into Jacob's room in the barn, but you know how stubborn Jacob can be. Sort of like another cowboy I know, and love."

The house was really no place for men that evening, or for that matter, for the next two days. The ladies were cleaning and cooking, like the king of England was coming to visit. I asked Clatilda if our house needed so much cleaning, how had we managed to live in it so long. Her answer was not to flattering to me, in particular, nor men in general.

That Saturday, folks started arriving by mid-afternoon and continued, as a steady stream, until long after dark. We had all been carrying Jacob high, but nothing compared to when he emerged from the barn in a brand-new suit, new boots and the fanciest chain, fob, and pocket watch I'd ever seen. He said it was an engagement present from Effie. When I asked him what he had given her, he only smiled and said I could wait and see.

There was no sit-down dinner. Just four or five tables groaning with every kind of food you could imagine, and it seemed every woman that came through our door, came laden with a dish of something, or a pie, or cake. I had visions of not having to buy groceries for the next three or four months.

Finally at eight that evening, Clatilda called everyone together and quieted the crowd, somewhat.

Jacob made the formal announcement of his and Effie's engagement and plan to marry in April.

"Why so long, Jacob?" one of the men shouted.

"I figure it will take me that long to totally convince Miss Effie that it's a good idea to marry me. And, if I waited any longer, I think she might see right through me. So, April it will be."

Then Jacob revealed his present to Effie. He pulled out a very nice Amethyst ring, and announced, that as it was the custom in more civilized countries, this was Effie's, 'engagement ring.'

Jacob took quite a ragging all evening over his remark about 'more civilized countries.'

Me? I spent almost the entire evening trying to see just how much hardware Jacob was carrying under his new suit. All I could positively identify was a knife hanging between his shoulder blades and possibly a pistol under his arm. I was positive about the knife, and pretty sure about the pistol. As far as Effie was concerned, well, let's just say, I didn't even want to speculate. Nor did my mama raise any children foolish enough to try finding out.

It was midnight before anyone left. And when they started, it was as if they vanished in the twinkling of an eye. It seemed one moment the house was full and the next, it was just our bunch sitting around the table.

Jess and Hester Turner were beginning to talk as if they would be leaving, when Jacob spoke up.

"Jess, aren't you the one who explained to Will about how the Church works?"

Most, around the table, looked at Jess. I looked at Jacob, and noticed Clatilda did the same.

"Yes, Jacob, I did."

"Well then, if I can get away sometime soon, I'd like to spend an afternoon with you," Jacob said.

"Come when you please, Jacob. As you know, I don't have a great demand for my time."

Things wound down after that, and within the hour Clatilda and I were alone in her kitchen.

"Will, do you think it's possible Jacob might join the Church?" Clatilda asked.

"I suppose anything is possible, but if John Terry thought I was rough around the edges, I wonder how he'll accept Jacob?"

"Oh, Will, you don't think there will be a problem, do you?"

"Not really, but I look forward to see how Jacob conceals his hardware with nothing on but a white shirt and trousers, when he's baptized."

Clatilda looked at me, and giggled. She was still, quietly, giggling when we went to bed.

The next morning, at the breakfast table, Jacob asked if I was serious about his building a house on the ranch.

"Of course we are, Jacob Webber. Where else do you think we would have you live?" Clatilda interrupted.

"She's right, Jacob. I thought you understood that," I said.

"Well, if its all right with you folks, I'd sure like to build in the edge of those quakies, just south of this house."

"That would be fine, Jacob, but only if you put Effie's kitchen on this end of your new home," Clatilda said.

"Well, that'll be fine, Miss Clatilda. But why?"

"So she and I can just step out of our kitchen doors and visit on the porch."

"Ma'am, you have neither a kitchen door, nor a porch outside it," I said looking at her in wonder.

"Not yet, cowboy, but I will have as soon as you get it built. And, if you're going to get it done before we go to Trinidad for your next court session, I'd suggest you get started!"

We did and after we'd laid the foundation stones for Jacob's house, we left Jacob, Jim Ballard, and Uncle Buck to get started gathering logs.

The trip to Trinidad was cold, but clear and pleasing. There were no such happenings as the last time I'd been there and, as we were becoming more comfortable with my position, the days were pleasant.

When we stepped out onto the hotel porch, the Monday morning of our second week in Trinidad, I looked down the street to see a cowboy coming at a wild gallop.

I turned to J.W. to comment, when something about the young man caused me to look closer.

"J.W., that's Bud!" I almost shouted.

I stepped off the porch as Bud swirled up to the hitching rail on a horse obviously ridden almost to death.

Bud swung down off his horse and made the few steps to where I stood, in one jump.

"Pa, you got to come home now. Uncle Buck's been shot dead, and Mr. Webber is in bad shape!"

Chapter 16

"Whoa, boy," I said, stepping down to put my hand on his shoulder. "Just slow down and tell me what happened."

"Pa, Uncle Buck and Mr. Webber had taken two wagon wheels to the blacksmith shop in town to get the rims fixed, and two fellows shot them. I don't know the whole story of what happened, but Uncle Buck is dead, and Mrs. Johansson says Mr. Webber will be lucky to make it. She and Uncle Seth says for you to get home and quick. And, Pa, I owe two ranchers 'boot' on horse trades I had to make."

"Don't worry about that son. Here," I said, handing him a small stack of double eagles, "go to Hawkins livery, down yonder, and have him get our buggy, J.W.'s horse and a horse for you. Bring everything back here. Can you do that, Bud?"

"Pa, I just rode better than halfway across the state, I figure I can make it to the end of the street!"

I looked at this young boy who was now a young man. My son.

I turned to J.W.

"Please go to the courthouse and make whatever arrangements are necessary. We'll leave for home as soon as I can get Clatilda ready and loaded into the buggy."

"Would you rather I stayed here, sir?" J.W. asked.

"No, J.W. There is family trouble at home. I want you there."

I will long remember the look he gave me as he turned to jog toward the courthouse.

I went up and quietly explained to Clatilda. Before I was half through she had begun to hastily pack our belongings.

Before we had completed carrying ours and J.W.'s luggage to the lobby, J.W. and Bud came into the lobby.

Within less than an hour after Bud's arrival, we were headed toward the mesa, north of Trinidad.

Bud was riding beside me, and I pressed him for a fuller accounting.

"Pa, I don't really know much. Thursday morning, Uncle Buck and Mr. Webber loaded two of the wheels from the hay wagon in the back of the spring board wagon, and told me and Jim they'd be back before supper. Then, just after dinner, Bishop Terry came beating it into the barnyard in our wagon. He had Uncle Buck and Mr. Webber on blankets in the back. Uncle Buck was already dead, and Mr. Webber was bleeding something fierce. I fetched Aunt Anne and she sent me for Mrs. Johansson. They fussed over Mr. Webber all night. Aunt Anne woke me up before daylight Friday morning and sent me after you and ma. That's about all I know."

"Didn't John Terry say anything about how it happened?"

"Nothing, except to tell Uncle Seth they had two gun slingers locked up in Mr. Webber's new jail, and you could take care of them when you got home."

"We'll have to see when we get there, I guess," I said.

It was not a pleasant trip back to our valley, and took longer than I would have liked.

We arrived late in the evening to find our home ablaze with lamps and lanterns.

Jess and Hester Turner were there, along with Effie Johansson and the Blalocks.

We had left Anna Laura to care for the twins, and when she saw her mother, she fell into Clatilda's arms sobbing about her Uncle Buck and Mr. Webber.

Seth took me aside and told me he wasn't sure Jacob would make it through the night.

Effie came to the kitchen, just as we came into the house.

"Will Jackson, please come with me. Would you also come, Uncle Jess?" she said turning to Jess Turner.

We followed her into one of our spare bedrooms, where she had placed Jacob. I was surprised to see Jacob's eyes open. He lifted one hand from the bed when I walked in.

"Will," Effie said, turning to face me and Jess, "Jacob has said few things since I got here, but the one word he keeps repeating is, 'blessing.' I believe he wants a priesthood blessing, and I wish you and Uncle Jess to administer that blessing."

I was not as surprised as I would have thought I would be, but we wasted no time, Jess and I.

That night will be long in my memory. It was coming on to full dawn when Effie came into the dining room, where we all waited.

"Will, Jacob is awake and would like to see you."

No preamble or even a 'by your leave.' It was as if he'd just come in from outside, and waited to discuss ranch business.

I walked into his room to find Jacob lying flat on his pillow, but wide awake. I walked up and laid my hand on his shoulder.

"Will, I've got to get something straightened out, if I'm not too late."

"Just lay back, Jacob," I said, "we've plenty of time now."

"No, Will. There were me and Buck, the two men that shot us, and the two that shot them. The two that took on the back shooters that got Buck and me were just waiting to get their horses shod. Will, I never saw anyone faster than the big one. There was him and the tall skinny one. Both were quick but, as I was going down I saw the big one draw and fire before the one who shot Buck could even cock his pistol and fire. And he was looking right at this kid.

"Will, I'm afraid folks thought those two younger men were involved in shooting me and Buck. They weren't, Will. No one will tell me. How's Buck?"

"Jacob, he didn't make it."

He said not a word, just turned to face the wall. I tried to ask him if he wanted anything, but he wouldn't answer me.

Effie finally laid her hand on my arm, and gently guided me to the door.

Everyone spoke up at once, as I returned to the dining room. I directed my answer to my daughter.

"Anna Laura, I believe your Mr. Webber is going to be all right."

She turned and grabbed her mother and sobbed quietly. This time it didn't hurt me to see my daughter cry.

We spent the rest of the day sitting around awaiting the periodic reports brought in by Effie. Jacob continued to improve even that short day.

The next morning J.W., Seth Blalock, and I rode into town to see John Terry.

When we entered the store, John came immediately to greet us.

"Will, good to see you. How is Jacob?"

"He seems to have turned the corner. He was even eating a little when we left this morning."

"I'm sorry about your Uncle Buck. When will you want to hold his service?"

"That's one of the things I wanted to see you about. Will tomorrow be all right?"

"What time?"

"We thought about two or three in the afternoon."

"That's fine. I'll take care of this end. Will you want to have it at your place or in the church?"

"That's good of you, Bishop. But, we figured to have it at our place."

"Done! I'll be there at noon. Now let's talk about this bad business we've got to deal with. I've got the two, that survived the shooting, locked up. We must decide what to do with them."

"I don't think so, John. Jacob says they were the ones that did for the two that actually shot him and Uncle Buck."

"But, Will, we have witnesses!"

"Did you take their guns, or did they surrender them?"

"Come to think of it, they both gave their pistols to Jim Barber, the smithy."

"Let's go talk to them. Maybe we can get the whole story."

We trooped down past the bank to Jacob's office, and the one cell. When we went in, I was surprised at the youthful appearance of both of the men in the cell. Neither appeared to be much older than Bud.

"What are your names, boys?" I asked.

"Me, I'm Festus Willberg and this here's Aaron Kennedy. We call him 'Judge'."

"Well, Festus, you want to tell me what happened at the blacksmith shop?"

"Yes, sir."

I waited, but so, also, did Festus.

"Well?" I asked.

"You mean now?" Festus asked.

"Yeah, Festus, I expect he means right now." This from the "Judge."

"Well, yeah, mister. Me and the 'Judge' were waiting to get a shoe tightened on the 'Judge's' horse when those two fellows came out of that saloon, next door, and just started blasting away at these two older men who were talking to the smithy. They never said nothing; just started blasting. Well, me and the 'Judge' figured that wasn't right, so we called them. That is, the 'Judge' called them. This one fellow he turned and told the 'Judge' to shut up, or he'd be next. The 'Judge' shot him. Then, when the other fellow turned on me, the 'Judge' shot him."

"What were you doing all this time, Festus?" I asked.

"Trying to get my gun cocked, so I could help the 'Judge'."

"You mean you can't even cock a pistol?" Seth asked, in wonder.

"Sometimes my right thumb sort of stiffens up. I have to pull it back till it pops, then it's all right for two or three days." Festus responded.

"That's sort of a bad problem for a fellow carrying a pistol, isn't it?" I asked.

"Yeah, sort of. But if I'm right serious, I can fan the hammer. I'm pretty good at that."

"Why didn't you 'fan' the hammer that day?" I asked.

"Didn't figure there was any need. 'Judge,' he already had his gun out, and there ain't nothing wrong with his thumb."

"Are you so fast, you figured to be able to stop two men, both of whom had their guns drawn?" I asked, turning to Kennedy.

"Yes, sir," was his terse answer.

"How is it, we've never heard of a fellow as fast as you seem to be?" Seth asked.

"We been down in the Nations. This is the first time we been in your town," Festus answered.

"What were you doing here?" I asked.

"We were headed home for 'Judge's' grandma's gold wedding anniversary. But we missed it, sitting here in your jail."

"Where's home?" I asked.

"Star Valley of Wyoming. Just up north, and a little east, of Salt Lake City."

"Son, isn't that mostly Mormon country?" John Terry asked.

"Yes, sir, just like here, but some colder, mostly."

"How do you know this is 'Mormon country'?" I asked.

"Sister Jennings, that brings us our meals, told us so."

"'Sister' Jennings?" I asked

"Yes, sir. That nice lady who comes twice a day."

"You called her 'Sister'," I said.

"Yes sir."

"Young man, are you by any chance Mormon?"

"Not by chance, sir. I reckon the 'Judge's' pappy meant it when he baptized the both of us."

I looked first at John, then at Seth. Frankly, I didn't know what to say next.

"Boys, do you hope to get off easier by saying you're Mormon? If so, you may be sadly mistaken. If we find you had anything to do with the shooting of our two friends, you'll find a Mormon neck stretches just as well as a gentile's," John said.

I looked at John. This was not the mild John Terry I thought I knew.

"Mister, I figure you're gonna do what you're a mind to with us. But you hear me, if you hang us it won't be for the killing of your friends. We didn't do that," Kennedy said, then turned to stretch out on one of the bunks in the small cell.

"He's right, mister. We ain't wanted nowhere, and for nothing. We tried to help your friends, but it appears you ain't interested in hearing the truth. Might be you'd want to have a talk with that Jubal in that there saloon. He probably knows more about the shooting than me and the 'Judge'."

So saying, Festus turned and climbed up on the upper bunk, over the "Judge." It was obvious both were through talking.

"Who is this 'Jubal'?" I asked of John.

"That would be Jubal Tyler. He's the one who owns the saloon. I don't know much about him, except he has become the bank's competition."

"How's that?" I asked.

"He had a big safe brought in and I'm told he's holding money for at least one of the bigger ranches southwest of here. He also runs sort of a pawn shop for his customers. I'm told his rates are pretty stiff. He'll loan you ten dollars, but you must repay twenty. And that within thirty days."

"That's got to keep a lot of those cowboys broke," I said.

"I do know that Jacob had a talk with him the week he was shot. It seems a cowboy from the Ladder Y claimed he'd been beaten, and his money stolen. Jacob told me Tyler had denied the cowboy's story, that the beating had taken place in the saloon. Tyler warned Jacob out of the saloon. Jacob said he'd just laughed at the man. and told him he'd come back when he pleased. You know Jacob."

"Yeah, I know Jacob. And now, I believe I begin to understand why Jacob and Uncle Buck were both shot in the back. Does anyone know who the men were who shot them?" I asked.

A muffled response came from the cell.

"What did you say?" I asked turning back to the cell door.

"Nothing!" Festus answered.

"Yes, you did. What was it?" I asked.

"I didn't say nothing!"

"Tell them, Festus!" the 'Judge' said, still lying on the bunk, and facing the wall.

"You think I ought to, 'Judge', what with them fixing to hang us, and all?" Festus said.

"Tell them, Festus!"

"Well, they was Ray Hudson and 'Curly' Benson. They was a couple of hired guns, from the Nations. We heard they were going out to Nevada."

"Do you know what they would have been doing here?"

"Nothing I know of, unless they was like me and the 'Judge,' just passing through."

"You said they came out of the saloon?"

When he didn't answer, I asked again.

Still no answer.

"Tell him again, Festus!" This from the 'Judge' who still lay, facing the wall.

"Yes, sir, that's what I said."

"Did they say anything before they started shooting?" I asked.

"One of them said Jubal said they was to get the two older ones."

"Do you remember exactly what they said?" I asked.

"Yeah."

I waited a moment.

"Tell the man what was said!" again the 'Judge.'

"Curly said, 'Jubal said get the older ones.' Then they just started shooting. That's when 'Judge' told them to quit."

"What then?" I asked.

"The 'Judge' shot them. I couldn't get my gun cocked. You see I got this bad thumb."

"John, I think I'll go have me a talk with Mr. Tyler," I said.

"Well, if you'll wait, I've get a friend, and we'll go with you," said Festus jumping from his bunk to the floor.

"I'll go with you!" the 'Judge' said, sitting up on the side of his bunk.

"Yeah, me and the 'Judge' will go with you, and watch your back."

I stood a moment looking at these two. They seemed no more than boys, but they were not.

Almost on an impulse, I stepped over and got the keys from where they hung beside Jacob's desk.

"Seth, are you armed?" I asked.

"I brought my shot gun. It's on my horse."

"John, where are these boys' weapons?"

"I have them in the store, Will. Do you really think this to be a good idea?"

"Do you have another? I don't know if I believe these boys, but I do intend to have a talk with Mr. Tyler." I turned to the cell.

"You say you are both Mormons?"

"Yes sir, me and the 'Judge' was both raised in the Church."

"Who is 'Brother Brigham'?" I asked.

"He isn't," tersely responded the 'Judge.'

"Oh?"

"No, sir. The man called 'Brother Brigham' is no longer alive. He was Brigham Young, the second President, and Prophet of our church."

"Do I have your word that if I give you your guns you will not use them, except as I say?"

"You bet! Me and the 'Judge' will do exactly as you say," Festus said, stepping to the cell door.

I stepped to the cell and opened it.

"Follow me," I said.

We went back into the store where John obtained their pistols.

As they strapped on their weapons I noticed there was nothing child-like in their actions.

The four of us, leaving J.W. and John at the store, rode across the bridge. We came up to the hitching rail, in front of the saloon, in a group. As we were tying our horses, I noticed a fellow get up from his perch on a bench, in front of the saloon, and disappear through the swinging door. I told Seth and the boys to step aside the door as I also stood to the side and, reaching over, swung the door open. I fully expected gun fire, but all was silent.

I stepped into the darkness of the saloon, then quickly to the side, away from the sunlit door.

Two men stood at the bar and a large baldheaded man against the back bar, wiping a glass. The man who'd gone in from the bench was nowhere in sight.

"Look out for our friend from the porch," I said to Seth.

"I'm looking for Jubal Tyler," I said, loud enough to be heard throughout the room.

"I'm Tyler. Who are you?" asked the bartender.

"Will Jackson; Judge Jackson to you, sir."

"You may be 'Judge' Jackson to that bunch of 'psalm-sayers' across the river, but you ain't no judge here!"

"You are so wrong, friend, I'll not even argue with you. I have only one question of you: why did you send that pair of worthless trash on their shooting spree?"

"What are you talking about?"

"I'm talking about Curly Benson and Roy Hudson. The two involved in the shooting at the blacksmith shop."

"I don't know what you're talking about," Tyler said slowly moving down the bar.

"Mr. Tyler, two things: First, stand where you are, and the second, you, sir, are a liar!"

The two men at the bar suddenly moved themselves away from Tyler.

"Festus, you and 'Judge' make sure those two fellows stand real still while I finish my business with Mr. Tyler."

I took a couple of steps toward the bar.

"Now, friend, let's you and I get this straight. All of your pals are going to be real busy so we won't be interrupted. Tell me, what made you think you could get away with such a raw deal?"

Tyler stood right still for just a moment or two then I could see, in his eyes, he'd made a decision. When he brought the scatter gun up from under the bar, I shot him twice. Both times in the face. He fell like a pole-axed steer.

"Boy, howdy, 'Judge'! Did you see that?" Festus shouted.

"Yeah, Festus, I saw it. I think maybe Judge Jackson was something else before he got to be a judge!"

"Yeah, and he's still something else. Man, I think he may be even faster than you."

"Festus, you don't say a lot that makes sense, but this time you are right."

I had turned to the two at the bar.

"You two," I said, "there was a fellow came in here just before we did. Where is he now?"

One of the men shuffled his feet. "Mister, there wasn't anyone come in here before you. No one in the last couple of hours."

"'Judge,' take that one outside and shoot him."

'Judge' looked at me for a moment, then turned, and taking the man's pistol and his arm, guided him past me toward the door. As he came by me, I slyly winked and he winked back. He was no more than through the door when we heard a thud, then a gunshot, and the sound of a body falling down the steps.

The other man was so anxious to talk he could hardly control himself.

"He's in that back room!" he said. "Right there. In that room there. Right through that door. He ran right in there after telling Tyler you were coming. That's where you'll find him. Right there!"

"Shut up!" Seth said. He then stepped to the door of the storage room.

"Mister, I've got a ten-gauge shotgun, loaded with double-ought buckshot. In about five seconds, I'm going to start shooting through the door and walls of that room. Do you wonder how many shells it will take to do you in?"

"Don't shoot! Don't shoot!" a voice came from the door. "I'm coming out."

"Throw your gun out first and come out with your hands high!" I shouted.

"I'm coming, mister, but I ain't got no gun. Please don't shoot."

Our man stepped through the door unarmed, as he said, and his hands high.

"Who are you?" I demanded.

"I'm just the swamper here, mister. I ain't mixed up in Tyler's doings. I was just to watch for anyone from across the bridge, and tell Tyler."

I looked the man up and down. If he was more than a saloon swamper, he could have fooled many. Me included.

"You own a horse, Mr. Swamper?" I asked.

"No, sir."

"Does Tyler?"

"Yes, sir. He has a grey gelding out back."

"Well, sir, you go put Mr. Tyler's saddle on his horse, and you get in that saddle and see if you can't get to Walsenburg before I change my mind and shoot you too. Festus you go with him and see that he leaves in a hard gallop."

"Yes, sir!" Festus said turning to the swamper.

"And Festus…"

"Yes, sir?"

"Cock your pistol before you go out there."

"Aw, Judge…" Festus said. But he drew and cocked his pistol before he and the swamper left.

"Now what, Will?" Seth asked.

"You know, Seth, I'm tempted to soak this place in coal oil and burn it to the ground."

"You reckon Tyler has any kinfolk?"

"I really don't care. They'd be hard put to cause any trouble over what has happened here."

"You know what I been thinking, Will?"

"What?"

"I been looking around ever since we came in here. This is one very solid building. This floor, being dirt, is the only slip-shod thing about the building. The rest is twelve inch logs and chinked real tight. This place would make a great warehouse. John's been griping about not having enough storage space, and I've sold potatoes to that broker in Pueblo, for two years, below the market because I had no place to keep them so to hold for a better price. That area down there at the end would be enough for me, and I'm sure John could make good use of this end. Is it possible to kind of confiscate this building?"

I looked at him for a moment, then laughed.

"Seth Blalock!" I said. "You're nothing but a pirate. And you a member of my own bishopric!"

Seth looked down at the floor and said, "I'm sorry, Will. I guess I let my greed get away from me. Forget I said anything."

"Forget it. Not likely, old friend. You and that ornery woman, of yours, have held it over my head for years about me running you off that 'homestead' you tried to set up. Now, you old pirate, I'm going to arrange for you and John to have this place. That's the least I can do for being able to call you an 'old pirate' for the rest of your days!"

"Now, Will, why don't we just forget it."

"No way, my old pirate friend. Even if there was not legal justification for what I'm going to do, I'd find a way. What's more, I'm going to write this whole thing down and give it to Bud. That way, if

I die before you do, he can pick up his heritage. Old son, this time I've got you!"

Seth tried all the way back to the store to get me to forget the whole thing. Festus and the 'Judge' couldn't figure out what we were talking about. But, I wouldn't explain, and Seth really didn't want to.

We placed, the men from the saloon, in jail while the four of us went to the store. As we were walking, I turned to 'Judge.'

"I heard a thud before the shot. What was that?" I asked.

"I didn't want him running or anything, so I cracked him behind his ear before I shot into the air."

"Boy, howdy!" Festus said. "I'll bet that'd give you a headache!"

"So he said," 'Judge' mused.

When we got to the store, John was waiting, anxious to hear what had happened. He said they had heard the shooting, but had waited to hear from us.

I explained the whole thing to him, including his new warehouse.

"Will, is that legal?" he asked.

"Just!" I said. "J.W. and I will draw up the papers. By this time next week, it will all be over."

I turned to Festus and the 'Judge.'

"You boys be leaving for Wyoming soon?" I asked.

"No, sir. We've missed grandma's anniversary so we'll be heading back to the Nations."

"You have work waiting for you?" I asked.

"No, sir."

"A girl?"

"No, sir."

"Anything?"

"Not really. Why you asking?"

I turned to John "You trust me, Bishop?"

"Completely!"

"'Judge,' how would you and Festus like to be our town marshal and deputy marshal? Won't pay much. About what a hand could make on an average-sized ranch. You can sleep in the jail, and I think John could be talked into furnishing you groceries. Right, John?"

"I think that would be no problem, only there would be one condition."

"What's that, John?" I asked.

"These two would be expected to regularly attend church."

"That a problem, boys?" I asked.

"Nope," 'Judge' answered.

"Shoot, no," Festus said, "and maybe we can get the 'Judge' to pass the Sacrament."

He sort of snickered when he said that.

"Festus, you shut up!" 'Judge' said.

"All right, 'Judge', don't get your dander up," Festus said, no longer amused.

"What's that all about?" John asked.

"Nothing really, Bishop," Festus said. "It's just a little joke between me and the 'Judge'."

"Shut up Festus," the 'Judge' said, again.

"Yes, Aaron."

"Then what do you say, boys? Do we have a new marshal and deputy?"

"Yes, sir. If you'll have us," 'Judge' said.

"Good! Then, we'll swear you in right now, and John will explain your duties. He'll not have you sweeping his store, but you are to do what he tells you. Is that understood?"

"Not you?" 'Judge' said.

"No, I'm just the town's 'gun hand,' right John?"

"Now, Will," John said.

"Seth, lets you and I go on home. We'll see you tomorrow, John."

"About noon?"

"That'll be fine."

We arrived to find Jacob sitting up in bed and getting, according to Effie, grumpier by the minute.

Jacob insisted, the next day, that he be brought to the living room for Uncle Buck's funeral services. We had expected few. There were many. And, it was after dark before all were gone.

The next day, Sunday, we once again found ourselves surrounded by well wishers. Festus and the 'Judge' were both there. Both scrubbed and shaved to within an inch of their lives.

The 'Judge' made a point of seeing Clatilda to apologize that he had been so slow in protecting Uncle Buck and Jacob. Clatilda responded by inviting him and Festus out for supper that night. He didn't want to come, and said he shouldn't. Clatilda responded by telling him to watch for us after services, and he and Festus could ride back with us, so they would know the way.

When we arrived at the ranch, Anna Laura took Festus and the 'Judge' back to see Effie and Jacob. She told us later that Effie had grabbed the 'Judge' and hugged him when he was introduced. Jacob shook his hand and thanked him, twice.

That was the evening, looking back, that I believe I lost my daughter. It seemed like any other evening at Clatilda's table. The family, guests, conversation, and, as always, teasing. Festus, it turned out, was quite a clown. He kept us all in a good humor with stories of his childhood. It seemed his parents had died when he was four and, for a couple of years, he had been shuttled from pillar to post, until taken in by Aaron's father. Rather than being hurt by the experience, he had found only the humor in his life. The only times he was serious was when he spoke of Aaron's father and mother. It was obvious they were special memories.

"Are your folks still living, Aaron?" Anna Laura asked, refusing to call the young man by his nickname.

"Yes, ma'am. Still living, and working their dairy."

"Don't you miss them, Aaron?" she asked.

"Yes, ma'am, but I feel I should be on my own."

"How long since you've been home?" Clatilda asked.

"Ma'am, its been almost three years."

"Miss it?" Clatilda asked.

"Yes, ma'am," he answered.

I changed the subject about the time Effie came pushing Jacob out in my office swivel chair.

"Will, I hope you don't mind. This old grump nagged at me until I couldn't stand it any longer. I hope our using your chair is all right."

"Of course! It's great to have you both in here."

She pushed Jacob up to the table beside me. She, Clatilda, and Anna Laura got up to get our desert. dried apple cobbler, and cream!

While the ladies were in the kitchen, Jacob turned to me.

"Will, my folks died when I was a little boy, and since then I've not lost anyone other than Buck's wife, Gladys, and of course, Cecilia Buckmaster. Does it get better?"

"The hurting?"

"Yeah."

"Not much, friend, not much."

He said no more. Then, or ever.

When the ladies came in with our apple cobbler, once again conversation became general.

We invited Festus and the 'Judge' to spend the night. At first they refused, saying they should get back to town, in case their services were needed.

Anna Laura insisted they stay, and play dominoes with her and Bud. Clatilda tried to not let that happen. I'd brought the game of dominoes into my family from my younger, wilder days. Somehow, Clatilda was uncomfortable with the game, but Jacob and I had spent many a cold night playing. The children, naturally, had learned.

It was interesting. Festus played fairly well, but Aaron, not at all. Anna Laura made it her crusade to teach Aaron so that by the evening's end he was holding his own, even against Festus and Bud.

By the time the game was over, two things were obvious: the four young people were fast friends, and the boys were spending the night.

They left for town right after breakfast.

As Clatilda and I stood on the porch watching them out of sight, Clatilda slipped her arm into mine.

"You know, cowboy, I always thought it would be one of the Blalock boys. I never dreamed it would be a stranger."

"Ma'am, what in the world are you talking about?"

"Anna Laura and Aaron Kennedy. That's what I'm talking about."

"What about them?"

"Didn't you notice?"

"What?"

"Anna Laura asked me last night if I didn't think Aaron was a lot like her Mr. Webber."

"So?"

"Will, you are a fine intelligent man, but you can be so dumb!"

"What are you talking about?"

"I believe Anna Laura is smitten by that Kennedy boy!"

"I hope you're wrong."

"Why?"

"He's not much. Just a young man with a gun and nothing to offer our daughter."

"Yes, much like a panhandle cowboy I met a few years ago."

"You don't really think Anna Laura is interested in him, do you?"

"We'll see!"

The next morning I was working with J.W. when we heard a rider gallop into the dooryard.

Aaron Kennedy and Festus were at the front door when I got there.

"Judge Jackson, we have a problem!" Aaron said by way of greeting.

"There's a couple of fellows over at the blacksmiths', saying they want to see you. They say they have a message for you from Cecil

Stewart. I don't know who this Stewart might be, but those two old boys aren't 'messenger' types. They're both wearing tied down holsters and riding real good horses."

"Did they say what they wanted?" I asked.

"No, sir. I didn't talk to them. Brent Salyer came over to the bank and told Mr. Terry. He told Bishop Terry and the bishop told me. It seems these fellows don't want to come out here to give you their message. They mostly want you to come to town and see them. I could have taken care of them, but I figured to talk to you first."

"Yeah! Me and the 'Judge' could have calmed those old boys down right sudden. But, we didn't know if they was friends of yours, or what." Festus said.

"Be quiet, Festus!" Aaron said.

"Aaron, I said, I do not believe I will be getting any friendly messages from Cecil Stewart. But I really don't understand these men being so open about everything."

"You want me and the 'Judge' to ask them to leave?" Festus asked.

"No, Festus, I think I'd better have a chat with these gentlemen."

As I went back into the house to tell Clatilda and J.W. I was going to town, I was in a quandary. Should I go to town as Will Jackson, Judge, or Will Jackson, rancher?

It came to me that while the two men in town had probably come to confront a judge, they probably could best be handled by a rancher.

I was getting my shell belt and holster, from my office, when Clatilda came in.

"What's wrong, Will?" she asked.

"It seems there are a couple of fellows in town with a message for me from Cecil Stewart."

"Isn't he the father of those boys who you tried in Alamosa?"

"One and the same."

"Do you think there will be trouble?"

"I can think of no other reason for their being here."

"Why not let Aaron and Festus handle it. It's their job."

"Ma'am, the 'message' they have is for me. I'll not start letting other people handle my problems. What if one of those boys got hurt, doing my dirty work? I'll not change the habits of a lifetime simply because there is now, some young man wearing a badge. A badge, incidentally, I pinned on him."

"Then please be careful, cowboy. I'd hate for Bud and I to have to go down in the San Luis and take on a bunch of rowdy ranchers."

"You and Bud?"

"Take a look at your son, sir. You'll see a man! And so much like you he makes my heart sing."

"Someday you're going to have to take him aside and explain to him why it is you don't love him very much," I said.

She slapped me on the shoulder, then reaching up, brushed her lips against my cheek.

"Be careful, cowboy, and hurry home."

When we rode into town, we were met by John Terry.

"Will, I was just going out to your place to warn you. Those two men have checked into the hotel and are just sitting on the front porch, as cold as it is. Will, they're waiting for you."

"Well, John, I'll not keep them long."

I turned to Aaron and Festus. "Boys, I'm afraid this is my problem. You'd best stay over here, on this side of the bridge."

"You firing us, Mr. Jackson?" Festus asked.

"No, son, but I'd not want to see you hurt over my problems."

"Then we're going, ain't we, 'Judge'?" Festus said, leaning in his saddle to face Aaron.

"Festus, there weren't ever any doubts," Aaron answered.

As we rode across the bridge, I told both I would try to handle the meeting quietly, but they should be ready for anything.

As sure as John had said, we rode up in front of the hotel to find two of the Stewart brothers sitting on the front porch.

I stopped my pony in front of where they were sitting.

"I am told you fellows have a message for me. I am Will Jackson."

"We know who you are!" one of the men said, as they both stood, stepping forward from the bench on which they had been sitting.

"Our pa said we was to bring you a message."

"All right. I'm here, let's hear it."

"It's just this, Mr. Judge. Pa says tell you if you ever come south or east of Saguache, you'll be dead before you get to Monte Vista."

"Did your pa have anything else to say?" I asked.

"No, sir. He just said to be sure you understood you were not ever again to come into the San Luis Valley."

Before he finished I had drawn my pistol and had it pointed at his shirt pocket. The surprise was plain on both their faces.

"Festus, you get down and take both these fellow's firearms. Be careful to check for hide-outs and knives."

In short order, both were disarmed and standing all alone on the hotel porch looking like they wished they were somewhere else, anywhere else!

"Now, Aaron, you think you and Festus can lock these fellows in your jail?"

"You just bet we can, Judge!" Aaron said.

"You put us in jail, and my pa will tear that jailhouse down around your ears!" said the one who had been the spokesman.

I sat there, on my horse, and thought for a minute.

"Aaron, you and Festus take this mouthy one to jail. Then you put the other one on his horse. If he's not completely out of sight by the time you can count to twenty, I'll buy a new Stetson for the one who shoots him out of his saddle. You," I said, looking at the quiet one, "go on back to your pa. You tell him I am issuing a warrant for his capture. Tell him I will put out a wanted poster on him. Those posters will call for his capture … Dead or alive!"

"Mister, you're digging your grave deeper and deeper!" said the talkative one.

"What's your name?" I demanded.

"I'm Lester Stewart, and this here's my brother Joe Bob."

"Well, Lester, it won't make much difference to you, one way or another, because you're going to be dead, anyway."

"What you mean, dead?" Joe Bob practically shouted.

"Why, man, didn't you know that threatening a judge is a hanging offense. I'd imagine with these two witnesses here, we ought to be able to have the trial tomorrow and the hanging the day after tomorrow. Or, at the latest, the day after that."

"Mister, you can't hang my brother. We didn't do nothing. We was just telling you what our pa told us to say," Joe Bob whined.

"Oh, shut up, Joe Bob. He ain't going to hang me. He's just trying to scare you!" Lester said.

I turned to Festus, "You got a good catch rope on your saddle?"

"Brand-new. Got it two days ago from Bishop Terry's store."

"You suppose that beam would be strong enough to hang a man from?" I said, pointing to an exposed beam over the porch steps.

"I'll just bet it would!" Festus said, stepping off the porch and retrieving his rope from his saddle.

"Now, my friends, understand this, I am the judge for this area and Mr. Kennedy, here, is the marshal. You are two strangers. If I hang old blabbermouth, here, who do you think is going to say anything?"

"You go get pa, Joe Bob. Whether I get hung or not, you tell pa to tear down this town and everyone in it," Lester said.

"That's right, Joe Bob, you go tell your pa. You also tell him I'll be in Alamosa a week from Friday. I'll be in my courtroom at eight that morning. If your father has not surrendered to Sheriff Hatcher by seven-thirty that same morning, I will dispatch a rider to the governor, and by Monday morning that whole valley will be crawling with state militia, and your father will be an outlaw. Now get on your pony and see if you can get out of sight before I change my mind!"

After we had locked up Lester, Aaron and Festus followed me out onto the board walk.

"Judge Jackson," Aaron asked, "can you really hang that guy for those threats?"

"Of course not! But it did make interesting conversation, didn't it?"

"Aw shucks," Festus said, "I was sort of looking forward to the hanging. I ain't ever seen one!"

"Shut up, Festus!" Aaron said.

"But, 'Judge,' you ain't ever seen one, either!"

"I said, shut up, Festus!"

"Oh, all right, Aaron."

Festus was in a funk for some time.

We went into the store, and I explained to John what had happened. I charged Aaron and Festus to keep a twenty-four-hour watch over Lester and to look out for any strangers coming into town.

"Will, do you think I should get some of the brethren to watch also?" John asked.

"No, John, I don't believe so. But, what I'd like you to do is have one of the young boys hang around the marshal's office, in case anything comes up. He could ride to the ranch and warn me."

"I'll see to it," John promised.

"It will only be necessary until a week from today. That's when J.W. and I will leave for Alamosa."

"Judge Jackson," Aaron said, stepping close, "how about Festus and me riding down there with you?"

"No, Aaron. I'll not take an army. There are too many now, who know the situation, for Stewart to really try anything. Stewart is a bully, but, like all such, he will realize his bluff has been called and wait for a better time. From now on the only question is whether he'll be on time with his surrender."

I went back to the ranch to find everyone awaiting my telling of what had happened.

When I had finished, Jacob said if I could wait an extra few days, he would go with me.

"No, Jacob, that won't be necessary," Clatilda said. "I'll be going with Will."

"No, ma'am, I think it would be wise for you to stay home this trip," I said.

Clatilda turned to Anna Laura and Effie, who were sitting side by side.

"Effie, may I add an extra burden to your day? I would like to leave the twins with Anna Laura. I would appreciate your watching over them all."

"That's no problem. I shall be here with Jacob, at any rate."

"Clatilda, I don't think this is a good idea. I would be more comfortable with you here. Besides, what could you do?"

"Kill the man or men who would harm you, cowboy! Kill them dead!"

There sat this sweet little Mormon lady. At her own table covered with a lace tablecloth, made by her own hands. Calmly, and sincerely, plotting murder. I loved this woman, but on occasion she was capable of making my blood run stone cold.

"Miss Clatilda, I have a couple of smaller pistols that would fit nicely in your hand bag." This from my friend Jacob, and him as serious as could be.

"Thank you, Jacob but I have Aunt Gladys' derringer, and I had John Terry order me a short barrel .41 caliber. Would you like to see it?" With that she removed from her apron pocket as mean a looking short gun as I've ever seen. From her apron pocket!

"What are you expecting, ma'am, Indians?" I asked.

"It seems I remember hearing of a man, whom I respect, once saying something about 'when one goes among the Philistines'."

Jacob slapped the table with an open hand and bellowed in laughter, such as could be heard halfway to town.

"Miss Clatilda," Jacob said wiping tears of laughter from his face, "you'll do."

From that day 'til the day he died, Jacob Webber was not again sick or feeble.

Chapter 17

The morning we left for Alamosa was a bright, cold day. Not a cloud in the sky so blue; it was like looking into a deep pool.

J.W. rode alongside the buggy. I had noticed that morning he had borrowed a saddle scabbard from Jacob and it now held a twelve-gauge double-barrel shotgun.

"J.W.," I asked, "why the shotgun?"

"I am not good with a rifle, sir, but one doesn't have to be an expert shot with a twelve-gauge loaded with double-ought buckshot."

"Well, be careful, friend! Whatever you shoot with that thing, you'll cut right in two!"

I turned to Clatilda. "Double-ought buckshot!"

"Well, J.W. is a careful man," she responded.

We spent the first night at the stage station in Saguache. I questioned Senora Maestas; she who had once thought to marry Jacob to her sister, about anyone who might have been hanging around the station.

She said there had been few travelers in the past two months and no one who had lingered beyond overnight.

The next morning we left and made a long day, arriving at the hotel in Alamosa just before nightfall.

When we went down the next morning for breakfast, the dining room was all but empty. I asked the man at the hotel desk to send a message to Jamie Nava that I would like to meet him in his office later.

After we'd had breakfast, I suggested that Clatilda might want to stay in the hotel.

"Cowboy, on this trip I'll be wherever you are, at all times."

"You wouldn't consider staying in the hotel lobby?"

"No!"

Jamie was waiting in his office when I got there. It took only a few minutes to relate the whole story to him.

"I'll have Sheriff Hatcher pick up Stewart before the sun sets this day!" Jamie said when I'd finished.

"No, Jamie, I sent the man word by his own son. I told his son to tell him when he was to turn himself in. I intend he should be given that chance. If he fails to show up tomorrow morning, that will be soon enough to send the sheriff."

We sat for a few minutes discussing the stupidity of the old man thinking he could pull off such a stunt. Jamie said he would have the sheriff's deputy stay close that day and, at least, the next.

"Will, what do you intend to do about Lester Stewart? You can't just leave him in your small jail. He'll eat your little town into the poorhouse," Jamie said.

"I've been thinking about that, on the way down here. I'm going to wait and see how this thing turns out with old man Stewart. If it's just another case of a loud mouth blowing off steam, I'll just let young Mr. Stewart, maybe, sweep some sidewalks, or paint the jail, or some such, then turn him loose. But if this thing down here is really serious, I'm afraid young Lester's punishment will also be serious."

"I'm concerned, Will. I don't believe I've heard of Cecil Stewart making idle threats. Just watch yourself," Jamie said as we rose to leave.

Clatilda, J.W., and I went to my office adjacent to the courtroom, to prepare the court docket for my stay there. It would be somewhat extensive as this was the beginning of my spring circuit.

We worked steadily until after noon. Clatilda offered to bring sandwiches from the hotel, and J.W. and I agreed.

J.W. and I continued to work and paid little attention to the time until I went in the courtroom for the water pitcher. I glanced at the clock and was startled to see it was almost two. Clatilda had been gone over an hour.

I was sure she had seen someone she knew, possibly Jamie's daughter, and got involved in conversation. But I didn't believe that Clatilda was the kind to stand around and gossip, when on an errand.

Of a sudden, I was very uneasy. I knew something was wrong. I told J.W. to shut down and come with me. I sent him to our room in the hotel while I questioned the waitress in the hotel dining room.

"Yes," she said, she had seen Clatilda, and wondered when she was coming back to pick up her order.

"Do you know where she went?" I asked.

"Not really," she responded, "She was talking to a gentleman, then left with him."

"Do you know who he was?" I demanded.

"I don't know his name, but he was that big-shot lawyer the Stewarts brought in when you tried their boys for killing those Padilla boys."

"Did you see where they went?"

"Not really, I was busy with the dinner crowd. The only thing was I saw them walk past the front window. The only thing I can say for sure is, they were headed east."

I rushed out on the street to see there were three businesses east of the hotel. A barbershop, saddle shop and a livery stable. I ran past the barbershop and saddle makers and into the livery stable. The hostler was cleaning stalls.

I asked him if a man and woman had been there in the last hour.

"Yeah, that Mr. Goodpasture from Denver and his wife left in a buggy about half and hour ago."

The description of Goodpasture's "wife" fit Clatilda, even to the color dress she was wearing.

"Did the woman say anything?"

"No, she was real mad. Mr. Goodpasture had to slap her a couple of times. I don't hold with no man hitting a lady, but seeing as how she was his wife, I didn't figure to get involved."

I turned to see J.W. standing at the door staring east.

I stepped out the door, and saw a buggy coming from the east. Either the team was in a runaway or someone was driving that buggy a lot faster than they should, particularly on a town road.

I was soon able to see the buggy was being driven by a woman. Clatilda!

She pulled the buggy to a halt in front of the livery stable.

"Will, this man needs a doctor, badly," she shouted as J.W. quieted the team. Lawyer Goodpasture was slumped down between the seat and the dashboard. The front and side of his shirt and coat were covered in blood. "I sent the hostler for the doctor, while J.W. and I laid him on a bench in front of the livery stable."

I cut off Goodpasture's coat to see the wound.

"Who shot him?" I asked Clatilda.

"I did, Will. I'm sorry but I couldn't reason with him and he slapped me, twice. I couldn't tolerate that. He said he was taking me to the Stewarts. I didn't intend to go. I had Aunt Gladys' derringer tucked inside my jacket, so when it was clear he'd stop no other way, I shot him and hurried him back so he could be seen by a doctor."

"You did well, Mrs. Jackson!" J.W. said. "But he appears to have been shot only once."

"That's right," Clatilda said.

"But, ma'am, if that's the derringer you showed me, it is a twin barrel .41 caliber."

"That's right, sir," Clatilda responded, somewhat quizzically. "Why do you ask?"

"Well, ma'am, I believe you'll find the opinion of most to be; that if you had two barrels, this man deserved them both!"

"Why, Mr. Fisher, I believe you are a bit bloodthirsty," Clatilda said, placing her hand on J.W.'s arm.

"It's just that no man should hit a lady. With any luck at all, the doctor will be out of town and the second barrel will prove to have been unnecessary."

Clatilda looked at me with shock on her face.

"Don't look at me, ma'am, I am in total agreement with my friend here!" I said.

The doctor arrived minutes later, and we took Goodpasture back to his office.

While he was working on Goodpasture's wound, the doctor turned to me, "Didn't I take care of one of your cowboys a few years ago? Seems I remember he'd been beaten very severely."

"Yes, sir, but he's well now. Got himself married and has started a fine little family."

"I don't know about this one. If he makes it through the next couple of days he might live. But it's going to be close. What happened?"

"My wife shot him."

"Intentionally?"

"Yes. He was in the process of kidnaping her."

"Kidnaping! I thought this fellow was the Stewart's lawyer. I hear he's been staying out at their place for several months. Nice enough fellow, I've heard, though I've seen him pretty drunk a couple of times in the hotel saloon."

"I still have trouble thinking Cecil Stewart would have sent him to carry away my wife!"

The doctor stopped working on Goodpasture and turned to me.

"You know something, Judge? I don't believe Stewart sent him. I've seen him a couple of times around that Stewart bunch. He seemed to be currying their favor. I don't know, but it just might be possible he thought what he tried to do would please the old man."

"There's too much about this whole thing that just doesn't fit," I said.

I took Clatilda and we went back to the hotel, where we found J.W. and Jamie Nava sitting in the lobby.

Jamie rushed over to Clatilda. He seemed less than even a little interested in me.

"Mrs. Jackson, if you'll just give me the whole story, we'll have that clan in jail before midnight!" Jamie said, holding Clatilda's shoulders in those ham-like fists of his.

"Hold up, for a minute, Jamie!" I said. "Doc Braden brought up an interesting point."

I explained the doctor's theory.

"I don't understand, Will. But, there may be something to that. I've been at a loss to explain why Goodpasture hung around here after the trial. From what I've heard, he had a very big practice in Denver. I know, when he came down here to defend Len and Buck Stewart, he came in style. You remember that outfit he showed up in that first day? Fred Pena, the bootmaker, told me Goodpasture paid him a hundred dollars for those fancy boots; can you imagine, a hundred dollars for one pair of boots? What has held him here, I don't know, but, he's hung around the Stewarts just like Doc Braden says. Almost like a puppy dog."

"I'll tell you what, Jamie, let's just wait until tomorrow morning. Stewart has been told to surrender to the sheriff by seven-thirty tomorrow morning and to be in my court by eight. If he shows, we'll get an answer, and if not, that'll be time of plenty to have Sheriff Hatcher pick up that crowd."

Jamie grudgingly agreed, but he said he would spend the rest of the afternoon arranging for Sheriff Hatcher to have plenty of company if it was necessary for him to go to the Stewart ranch.

J.W., Clatilda and I had a late dinner, then went back to the courthouse to finish our work there.

Twice, that night, I turned over to question Clatilda about details of her abduction. Both times she was sleeping like a baby.

We were all in the hotel dining room at six the next morning when Sheriff Hatcher and Jamie came in.

"Judge," Hatcher began, "I'll be needing a warrant, whether Stewart comes in voluntarily, or we have to go get him."

I handed the warrant, across the table, to him.

He glanced at it. "There's nothing here about your wife's kidnaping."

"That's right, Sheriff. I'm not sure, at this point, that Cecil Stewart even knew about that. He probably knows now, but I'll wait and see if he knew beforehand."

"But this warrant is blank where the charges should be shown!" Jamie said, having taken the warrant from Hatcher.

"That's right, Jamie. I haven't figured out whether to charge him for attempted murder or charge him under the old 'Vigilante' law."

"What's that?" Jamie asked.

"It's an old obscure law passed due to the trouble they had when the Central City Stamp Mills first got started. It states that it is a 'felony' to threaten an officer of a court with bodily harm."

"What kind of felony?" Jamie asked, setting forward in his chair.

"That's the beauty of it, Jamie, it doesn't specify. I'm sure if the law is seriously challenged, or appealed, it probably wouldn't stand up. But it's all I need to handle our friend."

"How in the world did you ever come across such a weird piece of legislation?" Jamie demanded.

"You remember when I was doing all that reading and studying before I hung out my shingle? Well, I just happened upon it, and it came back to me after we had the run in with Lester and Joe Bob Stewart up in Goshen. I thought I just might use it to bring Stewart down to earth."

"Will Jackson, you do beat all I've ever seen!" Jamie said, sitting back with a broad smile on his face.

"Well," I said, glancing at the wall clock, "I guess it's about time for us, all, to take our places. This could be a big day!"

Jamie left with J.W., Clatilda and me. We went straight to the courtroom to await whatever visitors the next hour might bring.

We'd been in the courtroom less than half an hour when the double doors burst open, and Cecil and Joe Bob Stewart, along with two rough-looking cowboys strode into the room.

"All right, Jackson," the elder Stewart shouted, "I'm here, when do you intend to hang us?"

All four of them pushed through the gate in the railing, separating the spectators section from the court. They were all armed, and appeared ready to use their weapons.

"I haven't made up my mind, Mr. Stewart, whether I'll try you, then have the hanging, or just go ahead and do the job today. What about it, boys, you think you'd like to hang today also?"

"You ain't hanging nobody, today or any other day. I sent word, by my boy, here, what would happen if you ever came back into this valley. Now, I aim to get it done!"

"Stewart, you know you can't get away with this! Why, man, if you go ahead with this foolishness, there'll not be a hole deep or dark enough to hide you!" Jamie said.

"You too, Nava! You should have hung that Padilla trash, and you didn't. I guess I'll take care of you too!"

The sound of, first, one hammer, then the other, of a double-barreled shotgun, being cocked sounded almost as thunder in the quiet courtroom.

"Mr. Stewart, Judge Jackson tells me that a twelve-gauge loaded with double-ought buckshot will cut a man right in two. From this angle I'd guess both barrels would get you and maybe two others. What do you think?"

Clatilda giggled! I'll swear, right there, in the middle of that mess, that woman actually giggled ... out loud.

Then Jamie Nava laughed. He was still chuckling as he disarmed the four would-be desperadoes. He was just finishing when Sheriff Hatcher and his deputy came in.

"Sorry to be late, Judge. I was waiting in my office when Doc Braden came in and told me he'd seen Stewart come in here."

"That's all right Hatcher. My clerk took care of the matter. It seems he had to add a couple of cases to the court docket. He, my wife and Judge Nava were having so much fun, we hardly noticed any problem."

"Sir?" The sheriff asked.

"Come on, John," Jamie said, "I'll explain after we get this bunch locked up."

The four were lead, docilely, out of my courtroom. Not a one had uttered a sound after the ominous cocking of J.W.'s shotgun.

"Now, ma'am," I said after they had gone, "just what did you see about that situation that was so funny?"

"Didn't you see?" she asked.

"See what?"

"The young man, Joe Bob? When J.W. cocked that shotgun, he started crying. I shouldn't have laughed, it was really pitiful. But the idea of them coming here to do what they threatened, then one of them tuning up to bawl, just like one of the twins, really struck me as laughable."

I looked at her for a moment, then turned to J.W.

"Friend, I love this woman, dearly, but should the occasion come along that you would think to borrow money from her ... don't!"

"Woman, you are one tough lady!"

That hussy just looked at me in that sweet innocent way of hers, then winked!

Chapter 18

It was said that there had never been such a turn-out for court in Alamosa as during that spring session. I think everyone showed up each day hoping not to miss the Stewart or Goodpasture trial.

J.W. and I plowed through the regular docket before calling the Stewart case. Stewart had hired a lawyer out of Pueblo. A gentleman by the name of Sajatovich. Mr. Sajatovich began the proceedings by demanding to know what charges his clients were being tried for.

Once again, I'd asked Mr. Tyson to prosecute.

"Mr. Tyson, will you please recite the charges, for Mr. Sajatovich?"

"Yes, sir. I left a copy at the desk in Mr. Sajatovich's hotel three days ago. However, they are as follows: attempted murder, kidnaping, felonious threats to a court officer, trespassing, carrying firearms in a courtroom, disorderly conduct, disturbing the peace and leaving animals loose on a public thoroughfare. It's my understanding Mr. Stewart and his son and employees left horses, untied, in the street in front of the courthouse." The last even Tyson could not keep a straight face while reciting.

"I received the charges Mr. Tyson left for me, but I had to hear them read in public. Your honor, this is the most ridiculous thing I've ever heard. What is this, some sort of a kangaroo court? I move for immediate dismissal of all charges!"

"Mr. Sajatovich, your motion is denied. As for these charges being ridiculous, sir, I personally signed the complaint listing each of those allegations."

"And you also intend to set in judgement?"

"No, as a matter of fact, I do not. I will recuse myself in favor of Judge Nava."

The trial, such as it was, turned out to be a real anticlimax. The jury quickly returned a verdict of guilty of the attempted murder charge, dismissing the other charges, as expected. Jamie sentenced Stewart to fifteen years in the State Penitentiary and released young Joe Bob and the two cowboys, with advice to the two cowboys, that they would probably find the Texas weather better to their liking. Joe Bob, was sent home, to take care of his mama.

There was, however, one interesting aspect of the trial. On the kidnaping charge, Sajatovich called an interesting witness: Doctor Orville Braden. As it developed, lawyer Goodpasture had acted on his own in the attempted kidnaping of Clatilda. The reason: his complete addiction to laudanum. It came out that when Goodpasture had first arrived at the Stewart ranch, to handle the defense of the Stewart boys in the killing of the two Padillas, he had developed a serious headache. Mrs. Stewart kept a supply of the opium derivative, laudanum, on hand and offered Goodpasture some. It allayed Goodpasture's headache, but it also addicted him.

Doctor Braden said Goodpasture must have been one of those rare individuals whose addiction was immediate and complete. There being no apothecary shop in Alamosa, Goodpasture had become completely dependant upon the Stewart's, for his drug supply. This explained his pitiful devotion, and his attempt to kidnap Clatilda in an effort to please his benefactors. Doctor Braden testified that Goodpasture was suffering much more from his withdrawal from the opium than from the wound inflicted by Clatilda. I agreed to not file charges against Goodpasture upon his promise to leave the area and a signed agreement to be forwarded to the governor that he, Goodpasture, would never attempt to practice law in the territory again.

As we were on our way home, Clatilda and I were discussing the whole mess when she turned to me.

"And after all of that, two families torn apart, all over a wagon load of firewood!"

Chapter 19

When we returned from Alamosa, construction on Jacob and Effie's new house had begun in earnest. Also, Clatilda's new porch was complete, facing the Webber home.

J.W. and I returned from the Trinidad court session, in late April, to find the house complete and Jacob's wedding date set for May first.

We were all sitting around the supper table one evening when Effie turned to me.

"Will, Jacob and I need your advice on some legal matters."

"Fine, Effie. After supper, we'll go back to my office and take care of them."

When we were all seated in my office, I could tell Effie was somewhat uncomfortable.

"Effie, what's the problem?" I asked.

"Will, can we have Clatilda come in here?"

After Clatilda was seated, I leaned back and asked Effie to begin.

"Will, as you may not know, I have a rather large estate, left me by my first husband."

She seemed to await my comment.

"I assumed as much," I said.

"Well, Jacob says he doesn't want it."

"Is this a problem, Effie?" I asked.

"Well, yes. What do I do with my money? I feel it's possible that Jacob and I, at our ages, will not have children, and if Jacob won't take my money, what do I do with it?"

"This is such a problem?" I asked.

"Yes, Will, it is. I can spend just so much buying trinkets for Jacob, and then the money just lies around, doing no one any good. I feel almost ashamed having it."

"Jacob," I said, "any particular reason you don't want any of Effie's money?"

"Don't need it. My herd is big enough that I can start selling off this fall. I have some money put by, and as long as you let me run cattle on your place, I just don't need Effie's money."

"Let me ask you something, Jacob," Clatilda spoke up. "Would you mind Effie investing her money, if she could find a worthwhile venture?"

"Course not. It's hers to do with as she pleases."

"Effie, why don't you and I go into the ranching business?" Clatilda asked.

"Ma'am, I thought you were already in the ranching business?" I asked.

"No, Will. You and Jacob are in the ranching business. And you also have your banking and judicial business. Effie and I are just expected to make cobblers, clean the house and look nice. You have always been just as bull-headed about my money as Jacob is about

Effie's. Effie, I don't know how much you have, but I can put up as much as might be needed for half of whatever venture we might take on. What about you?"

"Clatilda, let me just say that I have enough to be more than a little ashamed of just how much I do have."

"Will, would you object if Effie and I went into ranching?"

"Ma'am, I don't usually object to anything you do, but to ask me such a question is almost like asking how high is up? What, actually, do you have in mind?"

"Several things. First, of course, will be the land. You know that southwest corner of our place, down where the homesteaders tried to squat?"

"Yes."

"Well, that land butts up against the north corner of Jess and Hester Turner's place. Then just south of the Turner place is the Henson farm, and just west of that is the Widow Carstairs.' Now between those three pieces of land, there is over a thousand acres. If we took the Carstairs' place and raised hay, we could probably run upwards of four to six hundred head on the remaining land. And we wouldn't hold the calf crop to build a herd. We would sell every year, and by not bringing the calves through the winter; all we would ever have to feed in a closed winter would just be the mature stock. What do you think, cowboy?"

"It sounds like a reasonable idea. But I see two problems."

"What?"

"The land, and the hands to run your ranch and herd, not to mention working that four or five-hundred acre hay farm."

"I don't believe the land will be a problem, and you and Jacob can find the men for us."

"Just like that?"

"Well, not really, but Jess and Hester really can't work their place any longer, and if we were to buy their land and let them live in the house as long as they wanted, that would give us a little less than four hundred acres. The Hensons have been talking about how their son wants them to come live with him and his family over in Spanish Fork, and the Widow Carstairs has had her place up for sale for almost a year. I think we can buy all three properties for a right decent price. As for the manpower, I am confident you and Jacob can handle that problem."

"By the way, Miss Clatilda," Jacob asked, "where do you figure to get your stock?"

"I don't know, Jacob. I expect Effie and I will leave that to you, and Will."

"Let's see, now," I began, "you and Effie will buy the land. Of course I'll handle the legal work, then Jacob and I will buy and bring the cattle to your land, and find hands to work your ranch. Also, I would imagine you'd want us to locate, and buy, whatever equipment you will need on the ranch, and on your hay farm."

"That's about right!" Effie said.

"Tell me, ladies," I asked, "what is it that Jacob and I get out of this deal?"

"Why, that's simple, Will," Effie said, "you'll get the comfort of knowing you are not having anything to do with your wife's money."

"Effie," I said, "are you and Clatilda related somewhere back down the line?"

"What do you really think, Will?" Clatilda asked.

"How long have you been thinking about this, ma'am?" I asked.

"For sometime. The children are getting up where they can all take care of themselves, John Terry wouldn't sell me his share of the store, and you have your bank. Somehow a lifetime of hard work just won't let me sit in my kitchen and watch the bread rise. And, like Effie, I grow ashamed of the money that has accumulated over the years. It's only good for what can be done with it. What do you say, Effie, are you game to go into the ranching business?"

"It'll beat crocheting doilies. Let's do it. Let's go for it, Clatilda!"

"Of course, that's sort of like making bear stew. First, you have to catch a bear," I said.

It was decided that, instead of Jacob and I hiring some drovers and going out and bringing cattle to stock the new ranch, for which the land had not, even yet, been bought, we'd all go together. That is, Jacob, Effie, Clatilda, and me.

"But, first things first," Clatilda said, as we sat in my office. "We have the wedding to put on."

"What's to 'put on'?" Jacob said. "We'll go in and have Bishop Terry do the honors, then we'll be on our way."

"Ha!" Clatilda said.

"What do you mean, 'ha'?" Jacob asked sitting forward in his chair.

"Jacob Webber, haven't you even talked to Will?" Effie demanded.

"Well, I was going to. Probably tomorrow."

"No, my man! Now would be a good time," Effie said laying her hand on Jacob's arm.

"All right! Will, I'd thought to lead up to this, but it looks like that's not to be. I've been talking to Jess and Seth and, well, I guess I'd better get it done. Will, I'm going to join the Church, and I was kind of wondering if you'd baptize me this Friday?"

"No."

"No?" they all shouted at once.

"No! I'd kind of hoped if this day ever came, it would be in January, or maybe February."

"January or February?" Jacob asked.

"Well, at the very latest, early March."

"What in the world are you talking about?" Clatilda asked.

"Cold water, ma'am. I'd hoped for cold water. Real cold!"

"Mister," Jacob said, "for a fairly nice fellow, you got a mean streak that goes all the way through!"

"Of course, Jacob! It will be my distinct pleasure to baptize you. Oh, how I will enjoy dunking your worthless hide!"

"Let me tell you something, partner!" Jacob said. "I'll give you a quick count of three, then I'm coming up. You ain't getting my gal's money, by drowning me and taking one of them plural wives! No matter how much of an accident you might make it appear!"

Jacob and I both stood as I shook his hand, then we embraced, as brothers. This man, who had been so much to me, now to be even more!

"All right, then, Effie. Will you want to have the wedding Saturday, or next week?" Clatilda asked.

"Clatilda, do you think we could be ready by Saturday?" Effie asked.

"What's to be ready?" I asked. "Jacob puts on a clean shirt, and Effie washes her face!"

"Effie, let's you and I go into the kitchen. I think we can be ready by Saturday, but it will take intelligent planning. Obviously there's no intelligence that could survive in this room."

The ladies left and after some banter, Jacob and I got down to the discussion of where we might find cattle for the ladies' new CE brand.

Jacob's baptism went off as planned, and I was surprised when he asked Aaron Kennedy to confirm him a member of the Church. Even more surprised to find Aaron held the proper priesthood authority. That young man continued to amaze me.

I was Jacob's best man, and, Clatilda, Effie's matron of honor. Jess Turner gave the bride away. It was, by far, the fanciest wedding our little community had seen.

I was surprised Jacob didn't bleed all over his new suit. I've never seen a man shaved so close. I teased him some about it, but all I ever got from him was a silly grin.

We had a reception at our place that afternoon, and the party went on until late. Jacob and Effie escaped a little after the late supper, and while Seth and I and a few others wanted to shivaree the couple, Clatilda threatened dire happenings if we did. She was joined by Anne Blalock, and finally Hester Turner put an end to the talks.

"Will Jackson, if you do any such foolish thing, I swear I'll take a buggy whip to you." That brought a sobering note to the revelry. For the story was famous, and well told of how Hester had put an end to Jess' drinking when they were first married, and before Jess had joined the Church. It seems Jess had come home one Saturday night, very drunk and more than a little ornery. Hester had waited until Jess had passed out, then sewed him into a bed sheet. While Jess was lying there on his own bed, trussed up like a rag doll, Hester had taken Jess' own buggy whip and proceeded to thrash her own husband into a wide awake and completely sober state. Jess always claimed, though never showed, scars from the whipping. It was a story often told by

Jess and Hester. Always with a little humor, much love, and just a touch of irony.

So when Hester threatened a buggy whip, she was usually given proper attention and respect.

Sunday services, after Jacob and Effie's wedding, were great. Jacob and Effie were the center of attention, and while Effie was calm and a bit demure, Jacob was downright funny. He was proud of Effie, but more than somewhat taken aback by the amount and kind of attention he received.

Clatilda had invited the two for dinner at our house that evening. I think as much to test Anna Laura's reaction to the new couple as to honor them.

Anna Laura surprised us all. She and Effie seemed, in those few hours that Sunday evening, to become as close as if they had been blood relatives all their lives.

Clatilda told me that evening she'd not known what to expect, given Anna Laura's deep affection for Jacob. But, she said, not in her wildest dreams had she expected such a great outcome.

"Why, not?" I asked. "You raised her, didn't you?"

I often thought to remember that comment. It produced good things.

Chapter 20

Jacob and I began making preparations for our cattle buying trip by rounding up all the horses on the ranch to have them properly shod and working out some of the kinks from their being "pasture stock" for so long. We were met one morning, at the barn, by Effie and Clatilda.

"Will, Effie and I have an idea. We want to know what you and Jacob think of it."

"Yes," Effie said, "we've got a new idea, and we need your opinions."

If we'd had the sense God gave a goose, we'd have taken what horses we had and left in a high lope.

Instead, we just stood there.

"What we've been talking about is; Effie and I would go with you and Jacob. You see, we've been thinking we don't just want to buy a bunch of cattle, 'mixed stuff,' as you call it, Will. We want only mama cows, either bred, or open, and several good bulls. We don't want any steers or bull calves. What we've decided is; we want quality, not quantity."

"Clatilda, do you realize we could ride all over the territory and maybe a couple of other states before we could come up with the four or five hundred head, of the type of cattle you're talking about?"

"That far, Will?" Effie asked. "Surely, somewhere, there is some rancher raising the kind of cattle we want."

"That's just it, Effie," Jacob said, "they're raising, not selling. What you seem to be pointing toward is a lifetime project, not just an 'investment'."

"Will, there must be a way," Clatilda said.

"You know, Will," Jacob said, "there might be a way out of this. You remember that old boy down by Pueblo that bought your herd? Stanton was his name, I believe."

"Yes, Earl Stanton," I said.

"Well, when we were there, I visited some with his foreman. Stanton was upgrading his herd with some shorthorns he'd bought at the Denver stockyards. Said they'd come in from the northwest somewhere. He said Stanton was keeping some pure by breeding them only to shorthorn bulls, but he was also crossing some with longhorns. That old boy said Stanton was getting some prime stuff with that shorthorn cross. Could be we could deal him out of some breeding stock."

"Jacob, you want to think about what you just said?" I asked.

He looked at me for a long moment, then ducked his head and for a second turned beet red.

"Yeah, well," he said, "I guess we could just ride down and talk to my uncle-in-law."

We all laughed at Jacob's embarrassment.

"Jacob, I think that's a wonderful idea. It will be good to see my uncle and aunt again. Also, to have them meet my husband will be added pleasure!" Effie said, stepping over and slipping her arm through Jacob's.

Clatilda arranged to have Anna Laura and Bud watch over the twins and Seth and Anne Blalock to oversee the whole shebang.

We were as a bunch of children, that morning, as we left on our cattle buying tour.

As it turned out, it wasn't much of a tour. We all found exactly what we sought at the Stanton ranch. We were treated like family by the Stantons. Which, in fact, is what we were. At least half of our party.

Earl Stanton's first question of Jacob was if he now understood why we were referred to as 'Saints'?

Jacob's sheepish admission practically set the light-hearted mood for our visit.

Stanton not only had the cattle the ladies were looking for, but he was looking to sell. The dicker went much as my first experience with Stanton. He didn't get as much as he wanted, and we paid a little more than we'd hoped. Just as when I'd sold him my herd, at our first meeting. Only this time our roles were reversed.

Stanton told us we could either leave our new herd with him and come back for the cattle or he could loan us the drovers to take the herd home. That is, if we paid their wages both ways.

We discussed it and decided to take him up on his offer.

In order to do the job right, Jacob and I went into Pueblo and had a blacksmith make us a half-dozen branding irons. We brought them back, and Stanton, his crew, Jacob, and I had a busy week getting four hundred and twenty grown cattle branded.

When the branding was over, we butchered one of our cows and threw a big barbeque for the Stantons and their hands.

The subject of actual transfer of money to pay for the cattle never really came up, and the evening of the party, I apologized to Stanton and asked him if he would accept a draft on my bank in payment. He just looked at me sort of funny-like.

"Why, Will, that won't be necessary. Effie and Clatilda have already paid up. And, in gold too, I might add. I gave them the bill of sale for the cattle and bulls. They insisted the "bill of sale" list the number of cows and bulls separately. Said it would make their bookkeeping easier. And, say, you'd best watch yourself. Clatilda said she was going to charge you for the cow we roasted today. And, partner, she was only half joking! That's a pair you two have hold of. Somehow, as much as I think of them both, I'm sort of glad I don't have to deal with them and my Pearl on a daily basis. One of those three, at a time, is about all I can handle."

"Amen, brother!" Jacob said, having joined us early in the conversation.

"When will you all want to be heading out?" Stanton asked. "Pearl is anxious to have you stay a few days longer."

"I suspect we'll be leaving when the CE owners tell us," I said.

"Smart decision!" Stanton said, moving off to join others.

Fact was, we stayed a week. Jacob and I did little visiting, what with keeping our new herd separated from the Stanton cattle.

When we left Stantons, the herd, Jacob, five of Stanton's crew and I started out almost a full day before Effie and Clatilda. They caught up with us just about sundown, that first day.

After the evening meal, we were sitting around and I turned to Clatilda.

"Now, ma'am, please tell me, just how much gold did you and Effie bring?"

"More than we had to give Brother Stanton," she answered.

"Why didn't you tell me you two were packing around that sort of cash?"

"You'd have just worried and stewed. I guess as long as we are getting everything out in the open, we made an offer to Jess and Hester for their place, with the concession they live there as long as they please. They have agreed. We've also made an offer to the Hensons and the Widow Carstairs. The Hensons are thinking it over and the Widow Carstairs accepted our offer."

"You've been busy," I said.

"Why didn't you mention it?" Jacob asked of Effie.

"Jacob Webber, you told me time and again you wanted nothing to do with my money. If that's changed, say so. Little would please me more than to turn the whole matter over to you," Effie said.

"That goes for me too, cowboy," Clatilda added.

"Don't get me into this argument," I said. "I have only one question. That is, how's that money holding out? Are you going to be able to afford everything you'd hoped?"

"Oh, yes!" Clatilda answered. "And then some."

"And then a whole lot!" Effie joined in.

"So be it!" I said. "But, ladies, if and when we ever go on another buying trip, please let Jacob and I know if you're packing a lot of cash. Then when the road agents stop us, we won't look so stupid when you have to fork over a bundle of cash we won't even know you have!"

The rest of the drive went well, and when we got into the western edge of the valley, I rode on to the Medina's place. There I hired the whole family. Senor, Senora and both Medina boys. They would help with the balance of the drive, allowing the Stanton hands to be paid off and return to their ranch.

The cattle, by then, were well trail broke, and taking them on to our place was completely without incident.

Effie and Clatilda bought their land just as they planned. Jess and Hester were as happy as two newlyweds. They had their home and enough money to live out their lives in comfort. Jess had insisted on keeping the smaller of his two barns. He kept a milk cow, a couple of hogs and some chickens. Just enough to keep him and Hester going.

As I had hired the whole Medina family from over east of our valley to live on the Carstairs' place, the haying operation was taken care of. I told Senor Medina what Clatilda wanted done with the farm and turned it over to him and the various cousins, nephews, and other members of his family, whose names I often did not even know. He ran a few head of stock and consistently produced more hay than the CE could use, even in a bad winter. The Medina boys, Jamie and Al, worked on the ranch, year-round. They, their wives and families lived on the Henson place.

Clatilda and Effie were as good as their word. They drove cattle to Pueblo every fall and kept their herd at a steady four hundred head, give or take ten or twenty head.

Chapter 21

Aaron Kennedy became, more and more, a visitor at our home. He also, was always near Anna Laura on Sundays, before, during, and after church.

One Sunday evening, after supper, Clatilda and I were sitting in her kitchen. I was cleaning up the remains of a fine gooseberry cobbler, and Clatilda and Jessie were washing the dishes.

"Mama," Jessie said, "when Anna Laura and Aaron get married, can I have her room?"

I almost choked on my cobbler.

"What do you mean, 'when they get married'?"

"Yes, papa, when they get married. Anna Laura's room is bigger than mine, and it's got those pretty curtains at the windows. Besides Jake already has a bigger room than mine."

"Whoa!" I responded. "Who says Anna Laura's going to marry Aaron, anyway?" I demanded.

"Be quiet, Will. They'll hear you. They're on the front porch." Clatilda said.

"I thought Aaron had left an hour ago," I said, leaning back to try and see out the front door.

"If you'd get your face out of that cobbler, cowboy, you'd see a lot of things going on around you. I suppose you haven't noticed Bud mooning around John Terry's daughter, Martha?"

"Bud?"

"Yes, Will. It appears that, soon, it will be just us and the twins."

And so it was. Late in July, one evening, Clatilda and I were sitting on the porch when Anna Laura and Aaron came back from a buggy ride. While Aaron was tying the horses, Anna Laura came up on the porch and asked her mother if she could see her in the kitchen.

Aaron came up and sat down on the porch beside me. He sat there for a few minutes before saying anything. Finally, he turned to me.

"Judge Jackson, there's something I need to talk to you about."

"All right, Aaron."

"Well, sir, you see; I don't have much to offer. But, I'm a real hard worker and I promise, she'll never be mistreated or go hungry, or anything like that."

"Who, Aaron?"

"Why, Anna Laura, sir!"

"Are you asking to marry her, Aaron?"

It was long enough before he answered, that I finally turned around in my chair to more directly face him.

"Well, boy, I'll tell you, I'm not worrying about Anna Laura being mistreated or wanting anything. Should any such thing happen, it would be a close race to see who got there first; Jacob Webber or me. And should the guilty party have a choice, he'd be wise to hope for me and not Jacob."

"And just how do you intend to support Anna Laura, son?"

"Well, sir, Anna Laura tells me her mother and Mrs. Webber are looking for a foreman for their ranch. I intend to ask for the job."

"Can you handle it?"

"I know cattle, Judge Jackson. My folks not only ran a dairy, but we always had somewhere around a couple of hundred beef cattle. The country up there is a sight rougher than here. I kind of felt that would work in my favor."

"Well, it's a job you may be able to land. But if you do, who'd be our town marshal?"

"Festus."

"Could he handle it?"

"Yes, sir. Festus sometimes acts the clown, but that's mostly just to aggravate me. Festus is solid. And, if he gives you his word on something, you can forget worrying. He'll do what he says."

"Have you and Anna Laura spoke of when you'd marry?"

"I'd like to wait until I'm settled on a good job, but Anna Laura says if you approve, she'd like to get married before you leave on your fall circuit."

"And that's less than six weeks off."

"Yes, sir."

"Well, Aaron, I think there's a lot of 'ifs' involved in this thing, but if you can get everything tied down, and you love my daughter, I'll not stand in the way."

"Oh, papa!" Anna Laura shouted and ran out on the porch to grab and hug me.

"Hold on, Aaron still has to get a job to support you."

"No, he doesn't, papa. Mama says he can be hers, and Aunt Effie's foreman and she's already started having Brother Kedrick fix up the Henson house. She says it will be our wedding present!"

"What about the Medinas?" I asked.

"Mama says she and Aunt Effie will build them a place on the hay farm!"

Clatilda had stepped out on the porch and stood there looking at me, just like the cat that ate the canary.

"Woman," I said, "was there even a time you were not a step ahead of me?"

"Not that I'd ever admit, cowboy. Not that I'd ever admit."

That would have been all right, if it hadn't have been for Bud's announcement at breakfast the next morning.

Bud and Anna Laura had a double wedding the first Monday in September. Anna Laura to Aaron Kennedy and Bud to Martha Terry. Bud and Martha moved into the old cabin until we could get their house built.

Clatilda suggested I put Bud on our ranch payroll. By suggested, I mean, she gave me three double eagles the second week after Bud's marriage and said they were his wages, and I'd better give them to him, as she and Martha were going to town, that day, to get material to make new curtains for the cabin. That didn't make much sense to me. What with one store partner as her mother-in-law, and the other partner, her father. I didn't see Martha needing a lot of cash to get whatever she wanted in that store. But, nonetheless, Bud went on the payroll. He'd always been a good hand, only now I had to pay for his services.

That wasn't the worst of it, Jacob conspired, behind my back to set up Bud's own brand. He even sent to Pueblo for a couple of irons with

Bud's brand. Leave it up to Jacob to come up with something fancy. The Blue Cloud. Can you imagine! The funny thing was, it was only a B laying on the flat side. Branded that way it looked like clouds but, in reality, it was only a big fat, rounded, B lying on the flat side. Unfortunately, cowboys being what they are, Bud's brand soon became the Bumble B and was thus, forever known.

One morning late in April of the sixth year of Clatilda and Effie's venture, we were just finishing breakfast, and I was to leave that day to begin my spring court circuit.

"Will, we need to talk," Clatilda said as she began to clear the dishes.

"Well, ma'am let's talk. I can even leave tomorrow if you have a serious problem."

"Will, what if I asked you to postpone leaving for a month?"

"Then I'd postpone leaving for a month. You're serious, aren't you?"

"Yes, cowboy. I'm afraid I'm real serious."

"What is it, Clatilda?" I asked, even then almost afraid to hear the answer.

"Will, I went to that new doctor who set up practice in Goshen. He thinks I may be very ill. He wants me to go to a colleague of his in Pueblo."

"What's wrong, ma'am?"

"He's not sure. He says he thinks I may have a tumor."

I sat for a moment looking at this woman. I believe I'd never realized just how small she really was. She looked almost like a child sitting there across from me, that clear, warm spring morning. She had always seemed so sure and strong. There had been a few times in my life I'd not been absolutely sure I'd see her another day. Somehow the thought of Clatilda not being there never entered my mind.

"I will send J.W. to Alamosa, Trinidad and Durango. He will cancel this circuit. We will leave for Pueblo today. Do you suppose Anne or Effie can see to the twins?"

"That won't be necessary. I've already spoken to Anna Laura. She and Aaron will see after them."

"I thought they were going to Wyoming to see his folks."

"They'd talked about it, but she doesn't want to risk it, what with the baby due in another six or seven weeks. And you know how she is. Little Festus was almost two weeks early, and she says this baby is acting just like Festus did."

"Well, fine. I'm already packed. How long will it take you to be ready?"

"Just as long as it takes you to load my baggage."

The buggy trip we made to Pueblo, those next four days, was the most pleasant journey I've ever made. Even with the specter of Clatilda's illness in the background, we enjoyed the new spring greenery, and reminiscing over our full life together.

The doctor we saw in Pueblo confirmed what Clatilda had been told. I refused to accept his diagnosis and we left that same afternoon, by train, for Denver. Before we were through, we had seen four doctors in Denver. That made five doctors who each had confirmed the original diagnosis. The last four had echoed the prognosis given by the doctor in Pueblo. They each prescribed strong painkillers and said my Clatilda would probably not see another winter come to our valley.

I know I shall never forget that cold, blustering November day, when we placed my Clatilda alongside her children. In a coffin, I had fashioned the day before. I could have finished it weeks before. But until I held that lady in my arms, and she told me goodbye, for then, I could not believe I was losing her. I'd never considered myself a particularly brave man, but not a coward either. But those last few nights, I would sit bolt upright in the trundle bed beside Clatilda's and shake like a leaf in anticipation of life without my Clatilda.

After the services, there were those, including my own children, who wanted to stay with me. I refused their sympathy, or compassion, if you will. I wanted nothing more than to be alone in my home where Clatilda's touch was apparent in every room.

I sat alone in my office that afternoon, the day after the funeral, and stared, long, at the Indian rug which hung on my wall. I had never understood what she had felt that rug needed to be hung on a wall, but now I could not imagine it ever having been elsewhere.

I had dispatched J.W. immediately after the funeral, with my resignation from the bench. He was to deliver it directly to the governor. It was to be effective immediately and irrevocably. I told him he could then return, to live on the ranch, but he declined. I believed he, also, could not imagine the place without Clatilda.

It was hours past midnight before I finally decided what I was to do.

I went first to Seth and Anne Blalock, that next morning, finding them just sitting down to breakfast.

Both Seth and Anne tried to have me stay around for a few days, even weeks, to let the edge of my pain grow duller with time.

I went next to Jacob and Effie's where I gave Jacob my power-of-attorney to operate the ranch, along with Bud.

My only regret was the twins. They were both practically grown, and each a story of their own. Jessie, so much like Clatilda that to look at her in certain moods or movements, was to see Clatilda again. Little Jacob, now pushing six feet and strong as a bull, was so much like

Uncle Buck that I almost expected to see the old man when Jake turned unexpectedly. Both had been sorry that I was leaving, but of all, they seemed best to understand. I guess that the years of Jessie shadowing Clatilda, and Jake practically living in Jacob Webber's back pocket gave them a perspective of their old pa, the other children lacked.

Jake, particularly. He had been visiting with Jacob and Effie when I'd said good-by to them. He walked out to my horse, with me as I was leaving the Webbers.

"Pa, I rightly don't know why you have to do this, but I don't suppose I've ever known why folks do what they do. Pa, I'll be here when you get back. No matter how long it takes you to do what you think you have to do."

I stood there by my horse for a moment not thinking so much as feeling. Feeling with the raw emotion Clatilda's death had left me.

"Jake," I said, turning back around to face this man-son of mine. "How would you like to take a ride with your pa? We won't be back for supper, and I doubt you'll be putting your feet under any table like your Aunt Effie's for some time!"

"Pa, that would suit me right down to the ground!"

"Well, son, you get your horse and gear for light travel. If we need anything else we'll buy it. And, son, ride that grey you and Jacob have been working. You might need a good horse. You get your stuff together and meet me at the store in town by noon."

"I'll be there!"

Later that morning, I spent some time with Bud and Martha. Then I stopped by Anna Laura's. I spent an hour there.

Noon found me sitting in the bank offices with John Terry and Abraham Terry.

I gave Bishop Terry my power-of-attorney to function for me in the bank as well as the store.

As the sun was setting over the mountains, darkening my valley, Jake and I rode southeast into the San Luis.

Chapter 22

Jake and I camped that first night, just south of Saguache. As it was so late, we had only a small fire. The fire was more for company than for warmth. I'd picked up some bread and bacon at Terry's store, and we fried the bacon and then the bread in the bacon grease. While we were sitting by the fire with the last of our meager supper, Jake tried a couple of times to start a conversation, but I just didn't want to talk.

Finally, Jake turned to me, "Pa, I guess I can understand you don't want to talk much, but I was wondering, where are we going?"

"I don't rightly know, son. I don't even know if I will recognize it when we get there. I think, for a while, we are just going to be moving."

"Are we going to be riding the 'grubline'?"

"Where did you get that idea?"

"That's what Uncle Jacob said it looked like we were lining out to do."

"When did he say that?"

"When he was getting my stuff together to meet you in town."

I turned to face him. "Did Jacob give you any weapons?"

"He gave me a Smith & Wesson .44 caliber, a couple of derringers, and another knife. I already had my Winchester."

"What do you mean, 'another knife'?"

"Uncle Jacob gave me this knife four or five years ago." He said, pulling on a string hanging down the back of his neck. Out came a slender ugly thing. A six or seven-inch long stiletto, the duplicate of one Jacob had carried, for as long as I had known him.

"I know you can shoot a rifle, but how comfortable are you with that pistol?"

"Can I show you in the morning?" he asked. "I'm sort of tired tonight."

"Yeah, but it'll be the very first thing in the morning."

"Maybe," I thought, "that will help me to work on getting rid of this burden of self-pity, I carry now."

I slept little that night and was up, frying bacon and the bread, before the sun came over the mountain tops, to the east of us.

The sun was stretching its groping fingers of light across the night sky when Jake rolled out. He went immediately to his saddle bags and removed a shell belt and holster. After settling the belt around his hips, he dug out the .44 Smith & Wesson, and dropped it into the holster. I watched as he tied down the holster, around his leg.

"Son, you wear a tied-down holster, and someone is going to take you for a gun hand. Is that the picture you're aiming to paint?"

"No, sir. That's just the way I learned to wear it."

"Learned? Who taught you?"

"Uncle Buck and Mr. Webber."

"What else did they teach you?" I asked, looking at my son with somewhat different eyes.

"Well, Uncle Buck used to take me and Bud over by that old cabin, where you caught those boys who had rustled your cattle. We'd shoot for hours. Every time Uncle Buck could get into town, he'd pick up cartridges, then we would go over there. Uncle Jacob followed us once, and Uncle Buck swore him to secrecy, so mama wouldn't know."

"How long had that been going on?"

"Well, as I remember, about four or five years before Uncle Buck got shot. Then Uncle Jacob and I started back, almost as soon as he got well. Uncle Jacob had started teaching me to handle a pistol while Uncle Buck was still alive. Uncle Buck was the best rifle shot, but he said Uncle Jacob was the slickest man with a holstered pistol he'd ever seen. That is, with the possible exception of you. Pa, are you really that good with a pistol?"

"I'll tell you what I'm best at, son. That's knowing when not to use a gun. That's a right good-sized lesson, in itself."

We cleaned up our camp and after we'd saddled our horses, I turned to Jake. "Now young man, let's see how good you are with that sidearm."

"What do you reckon I should shoot at?" he asked.

"Pick yourself a target and have at it."

"What about that white rock out yonder?" he asked.

"That's not very ambitious," I said. "That thing's only thirty feet, or so."

"No, sir, I mean that one over there, on the side of the hill."

"Whoa," I said, "that's a little too ambitious. Boy, that's got to be at least a hundred, maybe a hundred and twenty-five feet away!"

"Yes, sir," he said.

I was still looking at the rock when it seemed to explode, simultaneously with a gun shot. I looked quickly at Jake. His gun was holstered and his hands were at his sides. I quickly looked around, thinking to see someone else. Seeing no one, I turned back to Jake.

"Once more, son. This time, try that near rock."

This time I watched as the fastest draw I'd ever seen was fashioned by my own son.

"Boy, did your Uncle Jacob ever tell you anything about your draw?"

"Yes, sir. He used to caution me about taking more time to be sure I hit what I was aiming at, with the first shot, but he hasn't said much about that lately."

"Jake," I said, "you are very fast, and more importantly, you are accurate. But, son, a word of caution; don't let anyone besides me see you draw and shoot."

"Why not, Pa?"

"You are fast enough to scare most people, and those you don't scare will want to test you. Then you will wind up killing someone or being killed, just over someone wanting to see if they are faster than you. There are two things I'd like you to do for me. Untie that thong from around your leg and don't ever shoot unless we agree it is necessary."

"What if things happen so fast you don't have time to tell me?"

"If they happen that fast, then use your own judgement. Son, just don't let yourself be goaded into showing off. Because, boy, you have a lot to show-off."

We mounted and headed south toward Del Norte. It was in my mind to head on across the mountains to Pagosa Springs, but after a bit we turned east.

Jake and I drifted on across the San Luis valley, sometimes riding with purpose, but mostly just riding. We stopped a couple of times for supplies, but mostly we made out with the occasional rabbit, deer. A couple of times Jake caught a mess of fish.

One night, we were camped just east of La Veta, and the subject of guns came up again.

"Pa," Jake said, "how does a fellow ever know how he is going to stack up against another fellow if he pulls a gun on you?"

"You don't. First off, try not to get yourself in a 'gun-drawing' situation. But, if it happens, there are only two considerations. First, don't think. That's the trick. If you think about it, at all it'll be over and the other fellow will be walking away. The second is training. You don't get to be good and survive a gun fight by simply drawing a pistol and firing. You have to train your reflexes in every way. Jacob used to tell me about an old boy he knew down in Texas who could catch two flies at once. Now that's quick, but it takes practice. And, Jake, you've got to act that quick and without thinking. To get so good you have to be comfortable with yourself and your weapon. I'm not that sure I ever want to see you get that comfortable with a pistol."

"Mama didn't think much of me having anything at all to do with pistols. She said there was coming a time when men wouldn't even carry them."

"That's probably true. But did your mother ever show you her arsenal?"

"No! You mean Mama owned a pistol?"

"Oh yes. She had a real shiny little two-barreled derringer that used to belong to your Uncle Buck's wife, Aunt Gladys. She also had the ugliest little short barreled .41 caliber revolver you ever saw."

"My mama!"

"Your mother."

"Did she carry them often?"

"I doubt she was ever without the derringer on her person. The revolver; well, only on occasion."

"My mama carried a gun!"

"Jake, your mother was a woman for the times. She was as comfortable in a church chapel as facing down armed men who may have intended to do her, or hers, harm."

"She sounds like Uncle Jacob!"

"If you'll think about it, you'll realize she was like a lot of people you know."

"Uncle Jacob always said you're plenty salty, yourself."

"Prepared, Jake, just prepared."

"Like Uncle Jacob says, 'when among the Philistines,' huh?"

Jake and I continued our wandering, south by southeast, mostly. We spent some time in Raton, at the southern foot of the pass of the same name. Jake liked it there, and we might have stayed longer, had it not been for the landlady in the boarding house we were staying in. She took it upon herself to match Jake up with her sister's daughter. I had no objections, but Jake found the match not to his liking. So one morning, we just saddled up and rode out. I'll swear, Jake looked over his shoulder 'til long after we'd crossed the Canadian River.

The pain I traveled with seemed not to lessen. Clatilda was seldom out of my thoughts, and although I seemed, almost hourly, to lecture myself about the self-pity I carried, I could not clear my mind of my loss.

Jake and I rode into Las Vegas, New Mexico one hot sunny afternoon. I had never thought to go there, but Jake had torn the sole from one of his boots and the rawhide thong he'd tied it back on with was itself now wearing out. We'd decided to treat both ourselves with new boots. So we sought a bootmaker. Las Vegas, we found, had two. The first did not have what we wanted, but the second had exactly what we sought. After our purchases, we were standing on the boardwalk, in front of the shop, when we heard a ruckus from around the corner. First, only loud voices, then shouting, followed by a single shot. Then there were three more shots, in rapid succession.

"This is a good time for you and I to find us a café," I told Jake. "One somewhere other than around here."

We'd taken no more than a couple of steps toward our horses, when two men came running around the corner straight toward us. At first I thought they were together. But it was quickly obvious one was chasing the other.

My knowledge of the Spanish language told me, quickly, they were not speaking kindly to one another.

They were no more than twenty or thirty feet from us, when the one in the lead stopped, turned, and blazed away at the other. The one in the rear quickly returned fire.

I'm not sure either could have intentionally hit the wall of a barn with a shotgun if they had been standing inside the structure. But they sure managed to hit my pony, twice.

I figured that was enough. I took a step back toward the boot shop to bring both in line, then I shot one in his right shoulder, high. The other, I shot right in his butt.

Neither was seriously wounded, but their yelling could have been heard all the way to Santa Fe.

In less time than it takes to tell about it, there were fifteen or twenty onlookers. Jake and I were kneeling, checking my downed horse when a tall, angular man pushed through the crowd, demanding of any and all to know what had happened. I heard at least three different versions from the crowd before I could even stand.

The two wounded men were being helped by some from the crowd, so I turned to the inquirer, whom I then noticed wore a badge.

"One of these fellows shot my horse. They seemed inclined to shoot everything in sight, except each other, so I figured to put an end to the whole thing."

"You shot both these men?" he demanded.

"Yes, I could have as easily killed both, but being stupid is not so much a crime as a shame. So I chose not to kill, just to put an end to their folly."

"You can't just go around shooting people in my town! I won't stand for it!"

"Look, friend, those two idiots shot my pony and just about everything else in sight, except each other. If you think I was just going to stand by until one or the other got lucky and hit me, you're wrong."

"Well, I'll just take your pistol, and we'll see what the judge has to say tomorrow."

"No, you won't," I said.

The man stopped, stepped back a step or two, and I believe, for the first time, really looked at me.

"Cowboy, you don't scare me. You may think shooting a couple of drunk kids makes you some kind of a pistolero, but, partner, I've eaten your kind for breakfast. Give me that pistol before I take it off your dead body."

"Mister, was I you, I wouldn't talk to my pa like that," Jake said, stepping slightly away from me.

"Well we got us a coyote, and his pup. Well, kid, I can take you and your daddy, so save yourselves a lot of grief and turn over those shooters."

"Jacob, take my rig off that pony. We'll be needing to get me another horse before we leave. Now, friend," I said, turning back to the lawman, "I'd always heard this was a right salty town, but if you're any example, maybe what I've heard was wrong."

"Cowboy, I don't care what you've heard, give me that gun, and right now!"

"All right," I said.

His eyes widened, for as I said, "all right," I had drawn my gun and had it pointed at his middle.

"Now, my friend, what comes now? You're not taking my gun for defending myself and my property. I'll go with you anywhere within reason. But, you're not 'taking' me anywhere."

"Cowboy, we got us a judge visiting from up north of here. Our judge died. You won't bluff him. You come with me, now, or I'll see you posted as 'Wanted for Attempted Murder'!"

"Jacob," I said, "you bring your horse and my gear. We'll go see this man's judge."

"What are you going to do about that dead horse, cowboy? You can't just leave him there in the middle of the road!" the lawman demanded.

"Your town's people killed him. They can dispose of him!"

We headed off toward the courthouse, him grumbling all the way.

When we entered the courthouse, he turned and looked at me.

"I don't know whether we'll find the judge in the courtroom or in his office. But, you just stick with me until we do. You tell your boy to stay close."

We went into a vacant courtroom, then back out around a hallway that seemed to circle the building. We eventually came to an office I guessed to be directly behind the courtroom.

The lawman knocked and was bid to enter.

When I heard the voice, I thought I recognized it. This was confirmed when we stepped into the office.

There sat my old friend and mentor, Judge Thomas Wagner, in his shirt sleeves, eating one of his regular dinner sandwiches.

He looked past the lawman, then recognizing me, he stood and came around his desk to reach out his hand, clasping mine, slapping me on the back in seeming jubilation at the meeting.

"Thank you, Deputy, for showing Judge Jackson to my office," he said, turning back to his desk, his hand still on my shoulder.

"Judge!" the deputy exclaimed.

Wagner turned to the man, "Yes, Deputy Perea, this is Judge Jackson from Colorado."

"Judge Wagner, this hombre just shot two men!" the deputy said.

"What is this, Will? What happened?"

"Two fellows got into a fight. They were shooting up the area right bad. They killed my horse and were in a good way to kill others, me included. So, I shot one in the shoulder and the other in his backside."

"His what?"

"He shot the man in his butt, Judge," the deputy said.

"Kill either one?"

"No," I said, "but one won't do much shooting for a while, and the other will be taking his meals off the mantlepiece for some time."

Judge Wagner smiled.

"This is serious, Judge. He could have killed both those boys. It's just dumb luck he didn't," the deputy said.

"Let me assure you, Mr. Perea, if Will Jackson had wanted those men dead, they now would be just that."

"Well, ain't you going to do nothing to him?"

"Yes, I think I am, Deputy. I believe I'll ask him to join me in my dinner. We have much to talk about."

"What about that kid?" Perea asked.

"Who's that?" Wagner asked, taking notice of Jake for the first time.

"My youngest son, Jacob, is with me. I believe the only time you ever saw him was in Trinidad when I was sworn in by Ralph Wheeler."

"Yes, but what I remember was a tow-headed young man not quite as tall as his mother's shoulder. I see young Jacob has grown a tad!"

Jake joined us, and while we ate, I explained about Clatilda's death and my leaving the bench.

"Will, was there no other way? I've heard so many good things about your court. Surely you could have taken a leave or some such."

"No, sir. I had to get away for a time, and I had no idea how long I might be gone. That's mainly why Jake and I are traveling together, so I would have a sort of tether, so I might not go too far afield."

"Even so, Will, I can think of few things more personally disappointing than to hear you've left the bench. Do you still intend to practice law?"

"Someday, but probably not soon."

We heard a knock on the door, and the deputy came back into the room.

"Judge Wagner, don't you think we should file some kind of charges against these two?" he asked.

"What would you have in mind, sir?" Thomas asked.

"Well, I kind of figured, maybe, attempted murder or at least disturbing the peace."

Wagner snorted, "Mr. Perea, there is a world of difference between attempted murder and disturbing the peace. Can't you settle on something more specific? And, I might add, a little more realistic."

"Well, what do you think we ought to charge them with?"

"I'll tell you what," Wagner responded, "let's charge Judge Jackson with discharging a firearm within the city limits and his son with aiding and abetting. How does that suit you, sir?"

"Is there a law against that there 'aiding and abetting'?" Perea asked.

"I'm sure there is. If not, there should be. Don't you agree, Deputy Perea?"

"Oh, yeah, Judge, that surely should be against the law!" Perea said, looking not nearly so sure as he sounded.

"So be it! Will," Thomas said, turning to me, "I fine you one dollar, and your son two bits. Please pay the deputy so that he may get you a receipt and close this matter. Do you understand, Deputy Perea?"

"I suppose, if that's the way you want it."

"That's exactly the way I want it, sir."

I handed the deputy a silver dollar and a quarter.

"I'll bring your receipt after a while," the deputy said turning to leave the room.

"You do that. Anytime within the next ten minutes will be fine," Wagner said.

After he was gone, I asked Thomas if he was having trouble with the man.

"He thinks that because he wears a badge and carries a gun, people should fear him. I don't. He seems to find that hard to understand. But enough of that. Tell me more of your family!"

We spent a pleasant hour or so talking. Thomas seemed genuinely sorry to hear of Uncle Buck's death and glad that Jacob Webber had finally married. About mid-afternoon, Jake and I took our leave. We spent the rest of that afternoon finding a horse to replace my dead animal.

Night found us camped south and east of Las Vegas. We'd found a quiet stream that cut through the pinons.

After we were settled down for the night, Jake turned over toward me. "Where are we headed now?" he asked.

"I don't rightly know. You have anywhere you'd like to see?"

"I don't know. I was just wondering where we might end up."

"I don't rightly know that we have a real destination. I just thought we'd see some country."

"You ever been down into Oklahoma Territory, Pa?"

"No, can't say I have."

"Aaron says that over toward Fort Smith, the country around there gets real lush and green. I've always thought I'd like to see that country."

"Why not! Let's head east in the morning."

"You mean it?"

"Sure, one place is as good as another to me. If you want to see Oklahoma, that's what we'll see."

Chapter 23

We loafed across the panhandle country and into western Oklahoma Territory.

After a couple of weeks, we started seeing the country turn greener. Not lush, but definitely an improvement over the country around the panhandle. We were riding across some right nice rolling country one morning, while Jake had been commenting on what good cow country we were in. I spotted a couple of riders top a ridge, then turn and head toward us.

"Jake," I said, "I never liked to see strangers change their direction and ride toward me. You be real careful, and while you're at it, slip that thong off your pistol."

I stepped down off my pony to better stretch my back and legs.

The two trotted up to stop about fifteen feet from Jake and me. They were as different as night and day. The older man was well-dressed and astride a fine animal. The other was in buckskins and blue ducking, sitting on a pony as stringy as he was himself.

"You boys just riding through, or you figuring to stop around here?" the well-dressed one demanded.

"We haven't made up our minds yet," I answered.

"Hunting work, country, or trouble?" the dirty one asked.

"Not really hunting anything, friend. But if we were, it wouldn't figure to be any of your concern."

"Hold it, a minute, cowboy! I'm Clifford Rayborn, and this pushy old goat is Abe Wilson, my wolfer. Not many wolves left in this country, but lots of coyotes, both four-legged and the other kind. I own the CR spread over south of here, and I was headed into Clinton to see if I could hire a couple of hands. If you boys are interested, you'd save me a trip."

"What do you say, Jake?" I asked. "You want to work for Mr. Rayborn?"

"Whatever suits you, Pa."

"Well, why not! Mr. Rayborn, looks like you hired yourself a couple of hands."

"We'll see if you are 'hands' or not," Wilson said.

"Mr. Rayborn," I said, stepping up on my pony, "we be working for you or Wilson, here?"

"You'd be working for me," said Rayborn. "Why?"

"Well, I just figured it's going to be hard enough working around this mouthy critter, and there's no way in this life I'd ever work for him!"

"What's your name?" Wilson demanded.

"Mr. Rayborn, I am Will Jackson, and this here's my son, Jake. As for you," turning to face Wilson, "when you talk to me, it had better be seldom and with absolute respect!"

"Get down off that horse, Jackson, and I'll show you how I'll talk to you!"

I looked at him for a moment, then the frustration, anger, and sadness of the past few months just exploded inside me. I spurred my pony, and in a split-second I was beside Wilson's horse. I grabbed the front of Wilson's greasy buckskin shirt. I jerked him toward me and hit him twice in the face. Then I jerked him off his horse down between our two animals. I piled right off right on top of him. I felt a burning sensation along my ribs and around to my stomach. I jumped back to see Wilson with a knife in one hand and a pistol in the other.

"Mr. Wilson, you'd better drop that gun!" Jake said, sort of quiet and low.

Wilson's eyes never left mine. "You'd best tell that kid of your'n to stay out of grown folk's business," he said.

"Mr. Wilson, this gun I have pointed right at your brisket is plenty grown-up, and if you don't drop yours, and right now, I'm just naturally going to kill you!"

"Not this day you..." Wilson started to say as he swung his gun toward Jake. I started to draw my pistol as I saw two bullets strike Wilson's shirt. One just below the collar and the second two inches below that first puff of dust.

Wilson turned toward me. "He killed me ... he shot me..."

"Friend," I said to him as he dropped to his knees, "he told you he would."

He then fell forward, his face splattering the dust from the dry grass.

"Son, you're in trouble. There wasn't any reason to kill that man!" Rayborn exclaimed.

"I should have just sat here and let him kill my pa?"

"It was just a fist fight," Rayborn said, weakly.

"Yeah, well, your friend had the sharpest fist I ever saw!" I said turning to show him my bloody shirt.

"Man, you're bleeding like a stuck hog! I didn't know he'd cut you." Rayborn said, jumping down off his horse coming around and handing me his jacket to press against the wound.

"Come on, let's get you to my house! My wife can fix that up."

He attempted to help me to mount my horse, but I shook off his and Jake's help and mounted by myself.

It was about five miles to Rayborn's place, by the time we got there I'd fairly well soaked his jacket with my blood.

Jake had loaded Wilson's body on the man's pony and brought it along. He appeared to be much more calm than I'd expected.

True to Rayborn's word, his wife was quite adept at patching wounds. She was also a good seamstress. She must have taken thirty stitches, closing the wound. Strangely enough, all the time she was working on me she was chewing Rayborn out something fierce. She kept saying she knew something like this would happen sooner or later and he should have gotten rid of Wilson 'long, long ago.' It wasn't until she had finished with me that she turned to Rayborn and asked where Wilson was then.

"Jackson's boy shot him," was his terse reply.

"Oh, you poor young man! Come over here and I will fix you a cup of tea."

Jake looked at me for help.

"Ma'am, we don't drink tea," I said.

"Coffee?" she asked.

"No, ma'am," Jake spoke up.

In an almost reticent manner, she then asked if her husband could get a shot of "spirits" for us.

"No, ma'am," Jake said.

She stood for a moment, looking at Jake.

"Young man," she said, looking over the top of her eye-glasses, "are you and your pa, Mormon?"

"Yes, ma'am," I said, "we surely are."

"Now, you see there Clifford Rayborn what kind of folks we are. That boy stood up for his daddy, and all, and you won't even read my Book of Mormon!"

She turned to Jake, "you come on over here young man. I'll fix you a big cup of hot chocolate. I bet your mama's made that for you more than a few times."

"Yes, ma'am," Jake said, as he eased past Rayborn and sat on the chair offered by Mrs. Rayborn.

Over the Rayborn's objections, I went outside and washed up and put on a clean shirt I'd taken from my saddlebag. Then I came back in and confronted Rayborn.

"Sir, is there a lawman in this 'Clinton' you spoke of?"

"Yes, there's a marshal, but he has only authority over what happens in town. There's also a sheriff, but he's drunk most of the time."

"Well, maybe we'd better go see them both. Drunk or sober, this thing needs to be settled. I'll not have this follow my son for the rest of his life."

Mrs. Rayborn tried to get us to wait until morning, but I insisted we leave immediately.

It was close onto dark by the time we got to town.

Finding the marshal was easy. But he told us, quickly, what we had was out of his bailiwick and not his responsibility.

We found the sheriff in a saloon, not yet drunk. We all told our stories, and he said it sounded like a clear case of self-defense, and he didn't want to be bothered anymore. That seemed to satisfy Rayborn but not me.

"Sheriff, I'd like you to convene a coroner's inquest, in order to officially establish my son's innocence. It is something I want to see established as a matter of public record. Not just a verbal dismissal."

"Cowboy, what do you know about 'coroner's inquest's'? What are you, some kind of a bunkhouse lawyer?"

"No, sir, as a matter of fact, I am a real lawyer, and I know quite a lot about coroner's inquests."

The sheriff, upset by having his drinking interrupted, left the saloon, in search of a magistrate.

By noon the next day, Jake, Rayborn, and I were on our way back to the Rayborn place. Jake had his release, signed by both the sheriff and the magistrate.

We spent a couple of days as the Rayborn's guests. That is to say, Mrs. Rayborn's guests. The Rayborns had no children and Mrs. Rayborn actually cried the morning Jake and I started back toward New Mexico.

We both agreed we'd seen all we wanted of Oklahoma.

We again took our time as we rode across that country. We wound up in Fort Sumner.

We were sitting in a café at noon, the first day in town when a fellow stuck his head in the door, and hollered he was hiring hands and anyone who wanted to work a roundup for the Walking Diamond should meet him at the Half Moon Livery in an hour.

Jake and I finished our dinner.

"Jake," I asked, "how would you like to work a real roundup?"

"Might be fun," was his response.

"Boy, let's get one thing straight. Working a real roundup is probably a lot of things, but I'll guarantee you none of them can ever be called 'fun'."

"Let's do it anyway, Pa."

And that's how Jake and I came to spend the better part of a year on the Walking Diamond Ranch. Hard work, and lots of it, and Jake did his share.

I watched this boy of mine turn into a tough, working cowboy. I also saw him become the sort of man Clatilda would have been proud of.

We never had a bit of trouble. Jake and I talked about Wilson only once. We were sitting out on a corral fence, one evening after supper when he brought it up.

"Pa, was I right in shooting Wilson?"

"Do you feel right about it?"

"Not really. But I just can't figure there was anything else I could have done."

"Well, boy, I'm going to tell you straight. I'm glad you don't feel right about it. Don't ever think you should feel right about taking another man's life. Even though, sometimes, the killing may be the right thing to do."

"It's not an easy thing, is it?"

"No, son, it is not. But what you did needed doing. You did it quick and took no pride in the deed, then or now. That's all that can be asked of any man."

We never spoke of it again.

Jake developed one vice, during our time at the Walking Diamond, however, he learned to shoot pool. About the only time we went to town, Jake and I, was on payday, Saturday, and that only happened once a month. Some of the hands had badgered Jake into playing pool with them. At first they tried to get him to play for money, but he refused. After a couple or three months, the badgering stopped. I heard one of the hands say he'd never seen anyone learn to shoot pool as fast as Jake, and, furthermore, there was no way he'd shoot with Jake for money.

Jake and I were sitting on the porch in front of the hotel, one hot August afternoon, watching a cavalry troop shuffle down the dusty street. They appeared to be as ambitious as we felt. We'd just finished a real good dinner, topped off with a big slab of apple pie. Neither one of us felt like doing anything more strenuous than just sitting, digesting our meal.

It was another payday Saturday afternoon, and so far Jake and I had spent exactly four bits of our forty dollar wages. Jake and I had worked for the Walking Diamond for almost a year, and each month we seemed to have more and more of our wages left over when payday came around again. We still had good rigs and our Las Vegas boots were still in good shape, and what clothing we'd brought into that country was still serviceable. We simply had nothing to spend our money on. I intended to spend another two bits that afternoon on a store-bought shave and haircut, while Jake was shooting pool, but right then, neither one of us had the energy to get on with our entertainment; him to his pool hall and me to my barber shop. Work was good, but when work was over, there was really little I cared to do.

I'd just about decided to go get my shave and haircut when, out of the corner of my eye, I saw a rider stop at the hitch rail. He dismounted, tied his horse and stepped up on the hotel porch. I stood and started to step around the man.

"Hey, ain't you Will Jackson?" the man said.

I turned to face him and noticed a vague familiarity behind his week-old beard.

"That's right," I said, "who are you?"

"I'm Lester Stewart, Jackson!"

"What do you want?"

"I want some getting even for the five years I spent in the pen, in Canon City! You can have it now or later, Jackson. But this day, I'm going to kill you!"

"Friend, you've made enough mistakes, in your life. Don't make another!"

"I'm walking out into the street, Jackson. If you have any guts, you'll come with me. If not, when I get to the middle of the street, I'll shoot you where you stand!"

He turned to face me.

"What's the matter, Jackson? You afraid to face me, without your gunnies to back your play?"

I watched, as if from afar, Stewart's hand swing down toward a pistol he wore in a tied-down holster.

He wasn't anywhere near fast enough. I stood on the porch in the hot sunshine of that August afternoon, and watched as one of his feet beat a tattoo in the dusty street.

Several men came running out of the hotel, including the town marshal.

I had already holstered my gun when the marshal demanded to know what had happened.

"He said he intended to kill me. I believed him, so when he tried, I shot. I was faster."

"Not in my town, mister!" the lawman said. "Mister you're under arrest! I'll see you stand trial for killing that man."

"But, marshal," Jake said stepping forward, "it was just like my pa said. It was a fair fight. That fellow called my pa out, then he started to draw first. It was a fair fight."

"This man's your father?" the marshal asked of Jake.

"Yes, sir."

"Well son, you better get your Pa a good lawyer, 'cause he's going to need one!"

Then he and a couple of bystanders grabbed me and after taking my gun, hustled me off to the town's jail.

I was locked snugly, in one of the two cells in the adobe jail. The marshal's deputy came by and assured me I would get what "I had coming."

I asked if he had seen Jake.

"The marshal says you ain't supposed to have any visitors until he says so. He ain't said so yet."

I laid down on the bunk, and finding it surprisingly comfortable, what with a nice breeze coming through the window, I promptly dozed off.

When I awakened, I was amazed to find it to be dark and even more taken by the fact that I was more relaxed than I'd been in months.

I glanced at the cell door and saw a tray of food on the floor, just inside the bars.

I ate with savor and was really disappointed there was so little.

After eating, I lay back on the bunk thinking to watch the starlit sky I could see through the cell window.

I was awakened by the morning sun streaming through that same window.

I had only been briefly awake when the marshal opened my cell.

"Get up, cowboy, and get out of that cell. A couple of punchers from your outfit and the captain from that cavalry troop all say you shot that fellow in self-defense, just like you and your boy said. I'll give you your gun back, but I want you out of this town. And, don't ever come back a-wearing it."

"Spend my money here but don't cause any trouble, right, marshal?"

"You got that right! Say, by the way, who was that fellow, you shot? He didn't have a thing on him besides eighteen dollars and change, plus a little old single-barrel derringer."

"His name was Lester Stewart, and his folks live up around Alamosa, in Colorado."

"You figure I ought to let them know? Could be they'd want to see his grave, sometime or something."

"I don't think it would make much difference to them. They have about had all the trouble one bunch can handle."

"You already had some trouble with that outfit?"

"Yes, you could say we have had our disagreements."

"Well, here's your gun. You'll find your horse in the livery stable. It'll cost you four bits to get him out."

"I'm sure the town had him well cared for."

"Well, I couldn't have him standing around all night. Somebody might have stolen him."

"Thanks a lot, for nothing," I said, accepting my gun and holster.

I walked out into the morning heat. It looked to be a scorcher, but I really didn't mind. For the first time in a good while, I knew exactly what I intended to do.

I retrieved my pony, found Jake in the café, and he and I rode out to the Walking Diamond.

McBride, the foreman wasn't real happy, or surprised, that we were drawing our time.

"Heard about your trouble in town, Jackson. Figured you'd be moving on. Did you get it all cleared up?"

"Yeah, I got cleared. Sorry to be leaving you so close to roundup, but I have business in Colorado."

We had ridden at least three miles from the ranch before Jake said a word.

"We going back to Colorado?"

"That's what I thought to do."

"You got business there?"

"You could say that. If you want to call my family my business."

"We're going home?"

"We sure are!"

Jake let out such a whoop that it took both of us five minutes to get our horses calmed down again.

Later that day, I had to finally tell Jake that if he didn't slow down we'd wear our horses out before we even made Las Vegas.

The sky was deep blue that Sunday afternoon, as we rode north. North toward our home. I wondered what John Terry would talk about in church that day. I thought, long, of Bud, and Anna Laura, and Jessie. I wondered if Anna Laura told her little Hester of her grandpa, and I wondered if Jessie had matured as much as Jake.

We were going home. I didn't know if I could live in Clatilda's house or ever again go into my office, but I was going back to my valley. I was going to walk up that hill and stand beside my Clatilda's grave. I thought I would not be real comfortable telling her about the past year and a half. Maybe, about like when I once before rode out on her, that cold blustery day.

I smiled to myself as I thought I'd have a chat with her. She never had given me that raise she'd promised.

No, no raise, just the grandest years any panhandle cowboy had any right to ever dream of.

As we rode over the next week or so, we watched the country change from a high desert to Pinon country then gradually into the high mountain country I loved so much. I had not realized how much I had missed that country. The quakies were green and alive with their movement, in the slightest breeze. They all seemed to be gossiping with one another while the pine and spruce stood stately and quiet, as if only mildly tolerating the constant, frantic gesturing of the never-still aspen leaves.

We saw deer, elk and all sorts of wildlife. The woods were never still. Once we surprised a big black bear robbing a bee tree. He looked at us for a moment, then decided the honey was more important. As we rode out of his sight, we could still hear him grumping.

One night, when we had camped along the Conejos River, Jake went fishing. We feasted on trout that night. It was so good to be back in my mountains.

Chapter 24

As we neared home, we chose not to go into the village, but instead, turned north to come into my valley from the northeast.

When we topped over the ridge, I saw the ranch laid out like a peaceful picture.

Cattle, horses, and kids. I could see them all.

Suddenly I was in a big hurry to be home. We trotted into Jacob and Effie's yard, by-passing my own.

Effie came from the house with a rush.

"Oh, Will!" she said, "welcome, welcome home! We have so missed you and Jake."

I stepped down, and she hugged me as her own. Then she turned to Jake and grabbed him in a bear hug. She then stepped back to look at him.

"Jake, you have become a man! Your mother would be so proud of you! Come on in, you two. Jacob's gone to town for Anne's medicine, but he should be back soon. He'll be so glad to see you!"

"Anne's medicine? Why didn't Seth go?" I asked.

"Oh, Will, you wouldn't know. Anne had a stroke in June, and she's been real bad ever since. Seth never leaves her side. The boy's put in his crop this year. Jacob goes to town for her medicine. It's been real bad."

"Effie," I said, "if you'll excuse me, I'll go on up to see her. Anne's always been special."

"Of course, Will, you go on ahead. You can see Jacob when he brings the medicine up there. Then you and Jacob get on back down here for supper, you hear?"

"All right, Effie, I'll see you later."

"How many more?" I thought, as I rode up to Seth's place.

I didn't bother to knock. Too many times had I been in this home to stand on such formality. As I had done so many times, in the past, I simply called out, "What's for supper?"

I heard a sound from the bedroom. Seth stood in the doorway. Tired, sad, and worn down. Not the brute of a man I'd known all these years. He strode across the kitchen, taking my hand in both of his.

"I told Anne you'd come back! I told her. Now, you're here!"

"Where is she, Seth?"

"Come on back, she'll be that glad to see you."

I walked into the bedroom to see a figure, in the bed, I barely recognized as Anne. I walked over and bent down to hug her. Her one good arm encircled my neck in a grip, surprising in one so slight. She held on, seeming unwilling to let go.

When, finally, Anne released me, I sat down on the side of the bed, whereupon she took my hand, and would not let go.

"Will, Will," she mumbled over and over again.

"She can't talk so good," Seth said. "Just a word or two, every now and again. She's called for you, lots. She seems to understand most of what I say to her, and she tries to let me know what she needs most of the time, but she's having a hard time."

"What can I do, Seth?"

"Just sit with her, Will. She's surely missed both you and Clatilda."

"Well, I can see how she might miss a handsome gentleman, such as myself, but if Clatilda was here, the two of them would be arguing over who was to do what."

I looked to see two tears coursing down Anne's face.

"Oh, I'm sorry, dear Anne, I didn't mean to upset you," I said, quickly.

"No, Will, she says you didn't," Seth said.

"How did she say that?" I asked.

"By rolling her eyes side to side."

Anne squeezed my hand.

"Oh, Anne," I said. "How great a friend you have been. You must get yourself well so we may once again enjoy your laughter."

We sat and whiled away the afternoon, Seth, Anne and me. It was just starting to get dark when Jacob came in with Anne's medicine. We excused ourselves, and I told Seth and Anne I'd be back the first thing the next morning.

As we rode back to Jacob's house, he told me more of Anne's illness.

"There was a couple of weeks, there," Jacob said, "when everyone, including the doctor, did not believe she would make it. You know, Will, she wanted her family around, but she was continually asking for you. She remembered that Clatilda was gone, but she seemed to feel you were around."

"We went through a lot, she, Seth, Clatilda and I. She is probably one of the best friends I've ever had. And, you know, even when we had the trouble with me trying to kick Seth off that supposed homestead, she was never bitter. She's one grand lady, Jacob. Right up there alongside my Clatilda and your Effie."

When we got back to Jacob's place, my whole family was there, including little Orson, Bud and Martha's baby, born in mine and Jake's absence. Effie had sent Jake to round them all up for supper. And, oh my, what a supper it was. I sat there at that table and looked around at the many people, including myself, that Clatilda had brought together. They ran the gamut from Jessie, so ornery and like her mother, it was frightening, to solemn Bud. Now, so much the responsible rancher, it made me proud. Actually the real son of two people I'd never known, but no less my own, than Jake or Anna Laura.

The evening ended earlier than I'd hoped, but my grandchildren had to be taken to their beds and as I told my bunch, I'd not soon go off sky-tooting again.

Most of the rest of that night I sat, alone in my old office trying to figure out what, now that I was home, I was going to do with myself.

I had much with which to concern myself. I had the ranch, the banks, the one in Goshen and in Monte Vista. There was Clatilda's ranching enterprise with Effie, and finally, Clatilda's share in John Terry's store.

I had no wish to have all these ventures hanging around my neck, plus I knew, if I chose, I could have a small, but solid, law practice.

By the wee hours of the morning I had made my decisions and went to bed for some of the soundest sleep I'd enjoyed since that stay in the Fort Sumner jail.

I was awakened, shortly after daylight, by someone pounding on my door. I knew who it was before I reached the door. It was Seth. I had only to look at him to know the reason for his early morning visit.

We buried Anne Blalock next to Clatilda on a bright, shiny fall afternoon. The weather fitted Anne. Clear, calm, a little cool, with a hint of the fall to come, in the air.

We held the services at my place, because I had more room and Seth thought it fitting. Seth's two boys, Seth, Bud, Jake and I carried Anne to her grave.

After everyone had gone home, I walked up to our little graveyard. Seth was also there. We, quietly stood together for over an hour. Neither of us had much to say. We just stood there, each lost in his own private little world of memories of the years.

It was getting on towards sundown when Seth reached over and placed his hand on my shoulder.

"Well, old friend, it's about time I got my milking done."

We parted then, each leaving a bit of ourselves in that small area, and also, the best parts of both our lives. Hard words we'd had, hard work we'd shared, women we had each loved, and children we'd lost. Those things, and the quiet respect for one another, seldom openly shown, but each, always aware. And, the love of one man for another, never shown, not shared openly, but there.

As I walked back down the hill, I was thinking I'd just left a dear friend that once I had thought to have to kill. My prayers that night were mostly of gratitude.

Chapter 25

I spent that fall rearranging my life.

I signed the home place over to Bud and Jake. I gave Clatilda's share of the CE outfit to Anna Laura and Aaron. I made sure that Jake and Bud understood that Jacob Webber's herd would be kept on the home ranch as long as he wished and that the Ballard's house and the Webber's house was to be theirs as long as they wished. Bud was, at first, a little leery of this arrangement. I settled the issue by making those wishes of mine a part of the deed, transferring the property to Bud and Jake. As siblings will, Jake and Anna Laura teased Bud about this. Bud, in his own way, took their teasing well. He was not, really unhappy about the arrangement, just a little uneasy until I put it in writing. Then his only comment was, "Good, now everyone is protected."

It had not occurred to me until then that Bud's concern was more for the Ballards and Jacob, than for himself. He then took another step higher in my estimation.

For my little Jessie, I signed over Clatilda's share of the store to her. Like Clatilda, this young lady had a head for business. The first thing she did was set apart the women's goods. The material, lace and such, into a separate part of the store, over which she established domain. John told me later he wished he had done such years before. He said the goods in "Jessie's department," as he called it, were the fastest moving in the whole store. I kept mine and Clatilda's bedroom set, which I moved into my old office. I moved my office to town in the new office I had built next door to Festus' jail.

The banks I kept, although I did arrange in my will to see that control of my share went to the children, equally, upon my death.

I then, quietly became a small-town lawyer. A few wills, the occasional property sale, and the rare litigation took most of my time. I did manage to sometimes make a nuisance of myself on one or the other of my children's ranching operations. Especially at branding and roundup times.

And, I must confess, Festus and I whiled away many a dull afternoon in his office. That young man, in spite of his occasional buffoonery, was a first-class chess player.

He taught me the game, and our sessions became a much anticipated part of my life.

We were so engaged one late summer afternoon when a rider stopped at the hitch rail in front of my office, next door to the jail.

"I hope he's not looking for me," I told Festus.

The man went into my office, and as I stood to follow, he came back out and started past the jail, when he appeared to spot us through the window.

He opened the door and entered, and as he did so he looked right at me.

"Are you Will Jackson?" he asked.

"I am, sir, what can I do for you?"

"Remember me?" he asked.

"Your face is sort of familiar, sir, but, I'm sorry, I cannot recall your name."

Festus pushed back his chair and standing, said, "I do, you're Joe Bob Stewart!"

"Yeah, that's me, and we just buried my pa last week!"

I don't remember what happened then.

But, it really doesn't matter.

Chapter 26

As I sit here looking over all Clatilda and I built in our lifetimes, I am amazed that one such as I could have had so much fun.

I remember Christmastime festivities, cold winters, long days of haying in the summer, the laughter, and oh yes, the tears of my children. I remember long evenings with friends. And, mostly, I remember the great days and the sweet nights with my Clatilda.

But, now I can't dawdle, sitting here looking at the ranch. For, there's my Clatilda in her red-wheeled buggy. She says I have an interview with Brother Brigham, so I'd better be getting along.

Adios, my friend.